Dear Reader,

Great news—in February 2013 Harlequin Presents Extra is merging with Presents so you will now be able to find more of your favorite authors in one place as Presents increases from six books a month to eight.

There will be more of the themes you love such as secret babies, marriages of convenience, scandalous affairs, all with exciting international settings and delicious alpha heroes. You can also look forward to linked books by some of your most-loved authors and a new exciting eight-book continuity starting in May.

So remember, starting in February there will be eight new Presents books available each month!

Happy reading!

The Presents Editors

Y0-AGO-659

P.S. Also available this month:

#3107 A RING TO SECURE HIS HEIR
Lynne Graham

#3108 THE RUTHLESS CALEB WILDE
The Wilde Brothers
Sandra Marton

#3109 BEHOLDEN TO THE THRONE
Empire of the Sands
Carol Marinelli

#3110 THE INCORRIGIBLE PLAYBOY
The Legendary Finn Brothers
Emma Darcy

#3111 BENEATH THE VEIL OF PARADISE
The Bryants: Powerful & Proud
Kate Hewitt

#3112 AT HIS MAJESTY'S REQUEST
The Call of Duty
Maisey Yates

"You presented me with unacceptable candidates."

"You really are being ridiculous. They weren't unacceptable. What's the problem? You didn't find them attractive?"

"They were attractive. But I was not attracted to any of them."

"You say that like it's my fault."

"It is," he said, whirling around to face her. His dark gaze slid down to her breasts and her own followed.

Jessica looked back up at him. "Elaborate," she said, teeth gritted.

"You expect that you can show up in that dress, and I can focus on other women?"

"What's wrong with my dress?" She gripped the full, tulle skirt reflexively.

"Other than the fact that you're showing off much more of your breasts than any man could be expected to ignore? It also shows your legs."

What Stavros was saying felt far too good. She wanted to turn it over in her mind, to savor it. To pretend that it was for her and that it mattered. To bask in being seen as pretty instead of broken.

Maisey Yates

AT HIS MAJESTY'S REQUEST

THE CALL OF DUTY

HARLEQUIN®

entertain, enrich, inspire™

Recycling programs
for this product may
not exist in your area.

ISBN-13: 978-0-373-13118-1

AT HIS MAJESTY'S REQUEST

First North American Publication 2013

THE CALL OF DUTY

When legacy commands, they must obey!

A Royal World Apart

Desperate to escape her duty, Princess Evangelina
has tried every trick in her little black book.
But where everyone else has failed, will her new bodyguard
bend her to his will?

Pity the Princess who draws such a devastating gaze!

Available in ebook!

At His Majesty's Request

Prince Stavros Drakos has ruled his country like his
business—with a will of iron!

And when duty demands an heir, this resolute bachelor
will turn his sole focus to the task....

But will he have finally have met his match?

This month!

All about the author...
Maisey Yates

MAISEY YATES knew she wanted to be a writer even before she knew what it was she wanted to write.

At her very first job she was fortunate enough to meet her very own tall, dark and handsome hero, who happened to be her boss, and promptly married him and started a family. It wasn't until she was pregnant with her second child that she found her very first Harlequin Presents® book in a local thrift store—by the time she'd reached the happily ever after, she had fallen in love. She devoured as many as she could get her hands on after that, and she knew that these were the books she wanted to write!

She started submitting, and nearly two years later, while pregnant with her third child, she received The Call from her editor. At the age of twenty three, she sold her first manuscript to the Harlequin Presents line, and she was very glad that the good news didn't send her into labor!

She still can't quite believe she's blessed enough to see her name on, not just any book, but on her favorite books.

Maisey lives with her supportive, handsome, wonderful, diaper-changing husband and three small children, across the street from her parents and the home she grew up in, in the wilds of southern Oregon. She enjoys the contrast of living in a place where you might wake up to find a bear on your back porch, then walk into the home office to write stories that take place in exotic, urban locales.

Other titles by Maisey Yates available in ebook:

Harlequin Presents®

CHAPTER ONE

"THERE is a science to matching people." Jessica Carter tucked a lock of blond hair behind her ear and lifted her computer, a flat, all-in-one device shaped like a clipboard, so that it obscured her figure. Pity, Stavros was enjoying the look of her. Even if she was starch and pearls, rather than spandex and diamonds.

She continued, her eyes never leaving the screen. "A matching of social status, values, education and life experience is very important to creating a successful, enduring marriage. I think most match services realize that." She paused and took a breath, pink lips parting slightly, her green eyes locking with his just for a moment before dropping back down. "However, I have taken things a step further. Matching is not just a science. It's an art. The art is in the attraction, and it's not to be underestimated."

Prince Stavros Drakos, second son of the Kyonosian royal family, and named heir to the throne, leaned back in his chair, his hands behind his head. "I am not so much concerned about the art, Ms. Carter. The essentials are general compatibility and suitability for my country. Childbearing hips would help."

Her pale cheeks flushed crimson, her lush mouth tightening. "Isn't that what all men want?"

"I'm not sure. And frankly, I don't care. Most men don't

have to consider the entire populace of their country when they go about selecting a wife."

But it didn't matter what most men did. He wasn't most men. Ever since he'd been forced to step into the place of his older brother, he had been different. It didn't matter what normal was, it didn't matter what he wanted. All that mattered was that he be the best king possible for Kyonos.

His methods might be unorthodox, and they might grieve his father, but what he did, he did for the good of his people. It just wasn't in his nature to be too traditional.

She blew out a breath. "Of course." She smiled, bright and pristine, like a toothpaste commercial. She was so clean and polished she hardly seemed like a real woman, more like a throwback from a 1950s television show. In Technicolor. "I… Not that I'm complaining of course, but why exactly have you hired me to find you a wife? I've read the newspaper articles written about you and you seem perfectly able to attract women on all your own."

"When I want to find a suit for an event, I hire I stylist. When I need to organize a party, I hire an events coordinator. Why should this be any different?"

She tilted her head to the side. Her hair was in a low, neat bun, her dress high-collared, buttoned up and belted at the waist. A place for everything and everything in its place. She all but begged to be disheveled.

Any other time, he might have done so.

"I see you have a…practical outlook on things," she said.

"I have a country to run, I don't have time to deal with peripherals."

"I've compiled a list of candidates, to be refined, of course…"

He took the monitor from her hand and hit the home button, tapping a few icons and not managing to find a list. "What is this?"

She took the device back from him. "It's a tablet computer. Shall I put that technologically savvy women need not apply?"

"Not necessary, but you can put down that women with smart mouths need not apply."

Her full lips curved slightly. "Someone has to keep you in line."

"No one has to keep me in line. I'm going to be king." That hadn't kept Xander in line. In fact, he'd pulled himself straight out of line and put Stavros in front. But Stavros wouldn't falter. He wouldn't quit.

One well-shaped eyebrow lifted upward. "Oh? Is that so." She typed something on her onscreen keyboard.

"What? What did you write?"

"Strong tyrannical tendencies. A possible negative in social interactions, possible positive in BA."

"BA?"

"Bedroom activities. It's shorthand. Don't dwell on it," she said, her tone snappy. "I told you attraction is considered. That said, do you require a virgin bride, Prince Drakos?"

"Stavros will do, and no, I don't." He shouldn't be surprised by her frankness. She had a reputation for being bold, brash even. She also had a reputation for setting up unions that had led to successful mergers and increased fortunes. She was a relationships strategist, more than a matchmaker, and he'd been assured that there was no one better. She knew the rules of society, knew the function a practical marriage served.

His marriage, and securing it, meant nothing to him personally, and being able to pawn off the legwork on Jessica Carter had been too good of an idea to pass up. And if the press happened to pick it up, all the better. He had a reputation for doing things differently. Doing things his way. Turning away from how his father had run the country.

And this was as far from something his father would do as he could think of.

"That's good," she said. "It's always awkward to ask women to submit proof of sexual history."

"Do you do that?"

"I have. Though not just women."

"Who?" he asked.

"Ah, now, if I told you I would have to kill you. I operate on the basis of strict anonymity. Unless those involved are seeking publicity, I don't talk about my clients."

"But word does spread," he said. He'd seen an old school friend three weeks earlier, and the smugness had practically been dripping from him as he stood there with his new fiancée. Oxford educated. And a model. She was everything he'd asked for. Beauty and brains. And who had accomplished the feat?

Jessica Carter.

The woman the media called the World's Most Elite Matchmaker. She catered to billionaires. CEOs, tycoons. Royalty. And she was renowned for making matches that lasted.

That was what he needed. He'd given up on allowing himself any sort of personal interest in the selection of his bride ever since he'd discovered that it was likely he would be assuming the throne for his absentee brother. His wants didn't matter. He needed a woman who could be a princess, an icon for his country, an aide to his rule. Aside from that, he had some of his own ideas. Someone beautiful, of course. Someone smart. Philanthropic. Fertile.

It shouldn't be too hard to find.

"This isn't just about me, Ms. Carter, this is about Kyonos. My family has seen too much tragedy, too much…

upheaval. I have to be the rock. I have to provide a solid foundation for my people to rest on, and establishing a solid marriage is essential to that plan."

The death of his mother, nineteen years ago, had shaken his people to the core. The abandonment of his older brother, the rightful heir, had caused months of instability. Stocks had tanked, trade had stalled, the housing market going into a deep freeze.

Why had the future ruler really left? Would he truly abdicate? What secrets were the Drakos family guarding beneath that veneer of polish and old world sophistication?

He had been determined to undo all of the unrest brought about by his brother. And he had done it. He'd revitalized Thysius, the largest city on the island, with posh hotels and trendy boutiques. He'd brought in new revenue by having the seat of his corporation on the island, a country much too small to house companies the size of his, when the owner wasn't the crown prince.

He'd done much to drag his country back from the brink. From the age of eighteen his entire life had altered so that it revolved around his homeland. He hadn't had the luxury of being a boy. Hadn't had the luxury of feeling fear or sadness. He'd learned early on that feeling had no place in his world. A ruler, an effective ruler, had to be above such things.

"I understand that this is a big deal," she said. "Not just in terms of your country, but for you. She *is* going to be your wife."

He shrugged. "An acquisition I've long known I would make."

Jessica let out a long, slow breath. "Mr....Prince Drakos, will you please stop being so candid? It's remarkably hard to sell a man who clearly has no interest in romantic love."

"Try this for a tagline—marry the jaded prince and receive a title, a small island, a castle and a tiara. That might make up for it."

"Money can't buy love."

"Nice. Trite, overdone, possible copyrighted by The Beatles, but nice. You might consider tacking this onto the end—love doesn't buy happiness."

Something changed in Jessica's eyes, a shard of ice in the deep green that had been warm a moment before. "That's for damn sure, but we're talking about putting together a sales pitch. And you aren't helping."

He shifted. "Can't you put something in my file about my impeccable table manners?"

"I haven't witnessed them, and I don't lie. You're my client, yes, but there is a pool of women I work with on a regular basis, and I have great loyalty to them."

It was intriguing. The way she flashed hot and cold. The way she presented herself, nearly demure, and then she opened that mouth. And such a lovely mouth, too. She was holding it tight. What would it take to make it soften?

The idea made his stomach tighten.

"And you think one of them is my queen?"

"If she isn't, I'll walk through all of Europe beating gold-plated bushes until a member of minor nobility falls out. I won't stop until we get this settled."

"You are supposed to be the best. You did manage to get a confirmed bachelor friend of mine to settle down."

"That's because, in my business, there's no settling. It's all about making the best match possible," she said brightly.

"Somehow, I do not share your enthusiasm."

"That's okay, I have enough for both of us. Now…" She looked back down at her tablet computer. "Your sister's wedding is in just a couple of weeks, and I don't want you going with a date, are we clear?"

He frowned. "I wouldn't have brought a date to a wedding." Weddings were where one picked up women; he didn't see the point of bringing one with him. The thought reminded him that it had been a very, very long time since he'd picked up a woman.

"And no leaving with any of the bridesmaids," she added. "You have to be seen as available, approachable and, oh yes, available."

"You said that already."

"It's important. Obviously, we don't want to put out a call for all eligible women in the kingdom to show up, so we need to go about this subtly."

He frowned. "Why aren't we putting out a call for all eligible women?"

"Look, Prince Charming, unless you want to put a glass slipper on a whole bunch of sweaty feet, you do this my way. That means you behave how I tell you to at Princess Evangelina's wedding."

"I wouldn't have picked up a bridesmaid. My sister's friends are far too young to interest me," he said.

"Ah…so you have an age range," she said, perking up. "That's important."

"Yes, no one as young as Evangelina. I'd say twenty-three at youngest. A ten-year age difference isn't so bad. Maybe cap it at twenty-eight."

She frowned. "Oh. All right." She looked down at her computer, then up, then back down again, her mouth twitching, like she was chewing on something. Her words, he imagined. She looked up at him again. "Why, exactly, is anyone older than twenty-eight too old?"

"I need a wife who can have children. Preferably a few of them. Any older and…"

"Right," she snapped, directing her focus downward again.

"If I ask you how old you are I'll only make this worse, won't I?" he asked dryly.

"I have no problem with my age, Prince Stavros, I'm thirty. Not that it's your business."

"It's not personal."

"I get it," she said. "And I'm not applying anyway."

"A pity," he said, noticing the way color bled into her cheeks.

Jessica set her iPad on the ornately carved table to her right and put her hands in her lap, trying like crazy to stop the slight tremble in her fingers. She was saying all the wrong things. Letting her mouth run away with her. Not a huge surprise since she tended to get prickly when she got nervous.

She'd managed to make that little quirk work for her over the years. People found her bold approach refreshing. And that suited her, since it enabled her to keep all shields up and locked, fully protecting her from people getting too close. Without showing vulnerability.

And now, with Prince Stavros Drakos, was not the time to let her guard down. No, most especially not with him.

"I've managed to finagle three wedding invitations," she said. "They will go to three girls that you and I will work at selecting sometime this week. At the wedding, you will speak to them for twenty minutes apiece, no more. And after that, I want you to pick one to advance to a higher tier. I've made a list of questions for you to consider asking."

"I'm not even getting a full date?" he asked, dark eyebrows lifting.

She shifted in her chair. He was so sexy it was unnerving. Because his aesthetic appeal couldn't be observed in the cool detached manner she might use to look at a nice piece of art. That was the way she'd been looking at men for the past few years. As lovely objects, nice to behold, but nothing that invoked feeling.

She'd let that part of herself go and she hadn't missed it. Until now.

Stavros…well, he made a spark catch in her belly. One that had been entirely absent for so long now she'd thought it had gone out permanently. It was a disastrous realization.

She stood up and took a step away from him, hoping distance would bring clarity. Or at least control over her body.

"You don't need a full date. Not at this stage. I've picked out a few candidates based on what we talked about over the phone. And now I've refined some of that, and I've got a number of women I'd like for you to have an initial meet with. You've been matched with them based heavily on compatibility. The kind we can establish from forms, anyway. Attraction," she said, the word sticking in her throat for some reason, "is actually one of the simpler parts of this stage. But it's not simple, not…not really." She felt her stomach tighten. The way Stavros was looking at her was intense, his brown eyes locked with hers. He was gorgeous.

It was sort of ridiculous how hot he was. It was as if he'd splashed around in the finest end of the gene pool, only collecting the good, the bad rolling right off. Square jaw, straight, proud nose and his lips…they changed a lot. Firm and unyielding sometimes. And other times, when he smiled, they looked soft. Soft and…kissable.

She swallowed and tried not to think about how very long it had been since she'd been kissed. She tried even harder to stop thinking about kissing Stavros's lips.

"Anyway," she said, breathing in deeply. She knew what to say next, knew her system by heart. She could explain it in her sleep. And she could take a few more steps away from him while she did it. "We start with that base attraction. What I call 'lightning bolt' attraction—" like the kind she'd felt when she'd walked into Stavros's office this morning "—or what many confuse with love at first sight. You'll feel a stronger pull of that immediate attraction to at least one of the women at the wedding. As we go on, we'll try and figure out which woman you feel a more lasting attraction for. But that's a different phase of the program."

"And you're accusing me of lacking in romance. You have this all worked out to a cold, calculated system. I'm not complaining, but let's be…what was the word you used? *Candid*. Let's be candid, you and I." A smile curved his lips and he rose from his desk, slowly rounding it. "You're no more romantic than I am."

His voice was like warm butter. It flowed over her body, so good, and so very, very bad for her. She cleared her throat. And took a step back. "All right, I'm not a romantic. Not really. I mean I was, at one time. But not so much now. What is romance? Warm fuzzies and the unrealistic ideals we project onto others when we're first beginning a relationship. Romance is an illusion. That's why I believe in matching people based on something concrete. From these basic principles, love can grow. And when the foundation is solid, I believe love can be real and lasting. It's when people go with that lightning attraction only, with nothing to back it up, that's when you have problems."

He lifted his arm and ran his hand over his hair, the action stretching his crisp dress shirt tight over his well-defined chest. She wondered what muscles of that caliber would feel like beneath her hands. She'd never touched a chest that looked quite like that.

Oh, dear. Wandering thoughts again. And redirecting…

"So, is that what you did?" he asked. "Follow one of those flash attractions, or whatever you call them, and have it end in disaster?"

She laughed and turned, hoping to look like she was

starting to pace and not like she was trying to put space between them. "Something like that." A lot more complicated
than that, but she wasn't about to get into it. "The point is,
I know what works."

"But you aren't married."

She stopped midstep, wobbling slightly on her sky-high
stilettoes. "I'm happily divorced, as it happens." Happily
might be overselling it, but she was rightfully divorced, that
was for sure. "I just celebrated my four-year anniversary
of unwedded bliss."

He arched an eyebrow. "And you still believe in marriage?"

"Yes. But the fact that my marriage didn't work helps
with what I'm doing. I understand what breaks things down.
And I understand how to build a solid foundation. You've
heard of the wise man who built his house on the rock, I
assume?"

"It's buried somewhere in the ether of my debauched
mind. Memories of childhood Sunday school lurk there
somewhere." Oh, he did that charming, naughty smile far
too well. It was no wonder he had a reputation as the kind
of man who could meet a woman and have her taking her
clothes off for him five minutes later.

She found her own hand wandering to the top button of
her dress and she dropped it quickly, taking another de-
fensive step back. He answered that move by taking three
steps forward.

She cleared her throat. "Excellent, well, I'm helping you
build a marriage on a rock, rather than sand."

His eyebrows lifted, one side of his mouth quirking into
a smile. He took another two steps toward her. "Different
than a marriage on the rocks?"

She stepped back. "Much."

"Well, that is good to know," he said.

"You and I will work together to create a strong partnership, for you and your country," she said, with all the confidence she could pull out of her gut. Confidence she didn't really feel.

He closed the distance between them and she took another step in the opposite direction, her back connecting with the wall. She forced a smile, and a step toward him.

He held his hand out, so large and tan and masculine. She just stared at it for a moment, trying to remember what one was supposed to do when they were offered a hand.

Her brain jolted into gear and she stuck her hand out. He gripped it, heat engulfing her as his fingers made contact with her bare skin. She wished now that she'd worn her little white gloves with the pearls. She'd thought them a bit quirky for a business meeting, but the shield against his touch would have been nice.

She just hadn't realized. Sure, she'd seen his picture, but a picture didn't do justice to the man. He was broad, nearly a foot taller than her, and he smelled like heaven. Like clean skin laced with a trace of sandalwood.

He made her feel small and feminine. And like she was losing her mind.

She shook his hand once, then dropped her own back to her side, hiding it behind a fold in her full skirt as she clenched it into a fist, willing the burning sensation to ease.

"I'll hold you to it, Ms. Carter. And I warn you, I can be a tough taskmaster."

Her breath caught. "I'm… I can handle you."

He chuckled, low and dark, like rich coffee. "We'll see."

CHAPTER TWO

"ARE you finding the accommodations to your satisfaction, Ms. Carter?"

Jessica whirled around, her heart thudding against her breastbone. Stavros was standing in the hallway of her hotel, a small smile on his face. "I... Yes, very. I didn't expect to see you here. Today. Or ever."

He looked around them, as though checking to see if he was in the right place. "This is one of my hotels."

"Yes, I know, but I assumed..."

"You assumed that I had no real part in the running of my hotels, casinos, et cetera. But I do. In another life I might have been a businessman." His tone took on a strange, hard tinge. "As it is, I divide my time between being a prince and running a corporation. Both are equally important."

She tried to smile and took a step back. "So, to borrow a phrase...of all the hotels you own, on all the island, you walk into mine?"

His sensual lips curved upward. It was hard to call it a smile. "Oh, this was calculated, but I also had a business reason for coming by."

Her stomach fluttered. *Down, girl.* What was wrong with her? A man hadn't made a blip on her personal radar for a long, long time. And Stavros was a client.

Anyway, she wasn't quite through licking her wounds.

The loss of her five-year marriage, and the circumstances surrounding it, had left her feeling far too bruised to jump back into dating. Which had been fine. She'd left her job, poured everything into starting her own company and perfecting her system of matchmaking.

Those who can't do, teach, those who can't find a match, match others.

That wasn't true. She *could* find a match. Had found one, back when she'd believed in falling in love accidentally with the aid of some sort of magic that might make it stick. As if it were so simple.

And then life had taken her dreams, her hopes, her beliefs and feelings, and it had jumbled them all together until the wreckage was impossible to sift through.

Until it had been much easier to simply walk out of the room and close the door on the mess, than to try and find some sort of order again.

But her ex-husband had no business wiggling into her thoughts. Not now. Not ever, really. That was over. She'd changed.

Her job had always seemed important. At first, being a matchmaker had been all about indulging her romantic streak. She'd been in love with love. With the mystical quality she'd imagined it possessed.

She knew differently now. Knew that relationships were about more than a flutter in your stomach. Now her job seemed essential in new ways. To prove to herself that it could still be real. That people could get married and stay married.

It was almost funny. She created successful relationships, successful marriages. And she went to bed alone every night and tried not to dwell on her broken one.

She'd had mixed success with that. But she'd had phenomenal success with her business. And that was what she chose to focus on.

"All right, what was your reason?" she asked, taking another step back.

"First off, I had to speak to my manager about handling all of the incoming guests for Mak and Eva's wedding. One of my gifts to them. Putting Mak's family up in the hotel. He could do it himself, and he's argued with me about it no end, but I'm insistent."

"And you do get your way, don't you?" she asked. She had a feeling he never heard the word *no*. That if a command was issued from his royal lips everyone in the vicinity hopped to obey him. It wasn't that he had the manner of a tyrant, but that he had such a presence, a charisma about him. People would do whatever it took to be in his sphere. To get a look from him, a smile.

He was dangerous.

"Always." The liquid heat in his eyes poured into her, his husky smooth tone making her entire body feel like it was melting. She was pretty sure she was blushing.

Oh, yeah, dangerous didn't even begin to cover it.

She cleared her throat, "And the other thing?"

"I came to get you. If you're going to be aiding me in the selection of my future bride, you need to understand me. And in order to do that, you need to understand my country."

"I've done plenty of research on Kyonos and…"

"No. You need to see my country. As I see it."

She really didn't relish the idea of spending more time with him. Because it wasn't really her practice to buddy up to a client, though, knowing them was essential. But mostly because, between yesterday and today, the strange fluttery feeling in her stomach hadn't gone away. The one that seemed to be caused by Stavros's presence.

"Are you offering me a tour?" She should say no. Say she had paperwork. Something.

"Something like that."

"All right." She wasn't quite sure how the agreement slipped out, but it had.

Well, it was best to agree with the one who was signing one's very large check when all was said and done with the marriage business. Yes. Yes, it was the done thing. So she really had no choice but to spend all day in his presence. No choice at all.

"Great. Do you need to get anything?"

"I was ready to go and have some lunch, so I think I'm all set." Her cherry-red pumps weren't the best choice for walking, but she'd packed some black ballet flats in her bag for emergencies. And anyway, they were amazing shoes and worth a little discomfort.

His eyes swept her up and down, a lift in his brow.

"What?" she asked.

"Nothing."

"What?" she repeated.

He turned and started walking down the hall and she clacked after him. "Why did you look at me like that?" she asked.

"Do you always dress like this?"

She looked down at her dress. White with black polka dots, a red, patent leather belt at the waist. It was one of her favorites, especially with the shoes and her bright red bag. "Like what?"

"Like you just stepped off the set of a black-and-white film."

"Oh. Yes. I like vintage. It's a hobby of mine." One her new financial injection allowed her to indulge in in a very serious way. Her bed might be empty, but her closet was full.

"How do clothes become a...hobby?"

"Because you can't just buy clothes like this. Well, you can, but they're reproductions. Which is fine, and I have my share, but to actually get a hold of real vintage stuff is like a game sometimes. I haunt online auctions, charity shops, yard sales. Then there's having them altered."

"Sounds like a lot of trouble for secondhand clothes."

"Possibly fourth- or fifthhand clothes," she said cheerfully. "But I love the history of it. Plus, they just don't make dresses like this anymore."

"No, indeed they don't."

She gritted her teeth. "I don't care if you don't like them. I do."

"I didn't say I didn't."

"Oh, the implication was all there."

He paused, then looked hard at her, his expression scrutinizing. "You know I'm royalty, yes?"

She nodded once. "Yes."

"And yet you still speak to me like this?"

She frowned, a slow trickle of horror filtering through her stomach. She wasn't backing down now, though—pride prevented it. "Sorry, my mouth gets away from me. Sometimes I need someone to restrain me."

He chuckled. "Ms. Carter, you have no idea how interesting that sounds."

Oh, but she did. Especially with the wicked grin crossing his lips. And it had been a very, very long time since she'd been with a man.

Longer since she'd missed it. Longer still since she'd enjoyed it.

"Jessica," she said, her dry throat keeping her from speaking in a voice that transcended a croak. "Just call me Jessica." Because for some reason when he called her Ms. Carter in that sexy, sinful voice of his, that Greek accent adding an irresistible flavor, she pictured him calling her that in bed. And that was just naughty. Naughty and completely out of the blue.

She wasn't interested in sex. Not the responsibility of it, not the repercussions of it. And not the pain that resulted from it.

"Jessica," he said, slowly, like he was tasting it.

Well, that didn't help, either.

"Prince Stavros?"

"Stavros. Please."

Her heart pattered, a sort of irregular beat, like it had tripped. "I don't assume you're in the habit of asking commoners to call you by your first name?"

He shrugged. "Titles are fine. In many regards, they are necessary as they establish one's place in society. I like them for negotiation, for the media. I don't really like them in conversation."

"All right then," she said, "Stavros." She put a lot of effort into the name, taking her time to savor the syllables, as he'd done to hers. She saw a flicker of heat in his dark eyes and fought to ignore an answering flame that ignited in her stomach.

"We'll start here," he said, indicating the halls of the hotel as he began to walk ahead. "This hotel, and many others like it, have been essential to my country. After the death of my mother, my father started neglecting the tourism industry. He neglected a great many things. I was fourteen at the time. My brother, the heir to the throne, was sixteen. He left a few years after that. It became clear that Xander was gone, and that we could not count on him to see to his duties." Stavros didn't bother to hide the hint of bitterness in his voice. "That started rumors of civil unrest. And of course tourists don't want to be somewhere that could possibly be dangerous. As soon as I was able I did what I could to start a revival of the tourism industry. I went abroad for college, established contacts. I studied business, hospitality, economics. Whatever I thought might be helpful in getting my country back to where it needed to be."

"You turned Kyonos into a business."

"Essentially. But not for my own gain. For the gain of my people."

"True," she said, "but by all accounts you have gained quite a bit."

"I have. I won't lie. My own bank account is healthy, in part due to the fact that, at this point, the interest it's collecting on a yearly basis is more than most people will see in a lifetime." He turned to look at her. "Do you need my estimated net worth for your records so you can pass it on to the women you're considering for me?"

"What? Oh, no. I think they'll feel secure enough in your…assets. I doubt they'll need anything so crass as actual net worth. A ballpark figure will do."

"You're very honest."

"Yes, well." She took in a deep breath and tried to ignore the tightening in her stomach. "Hiding from reality doesn't fix anything."

"No. It doesn't," he said.

She could tell, from the icy tone in his voice, the depth to each word, that he was speaking from experience. Just like her.

Interesting that she could fly halfway across the world and meet a prince who seemed to have more common ground with her than anyone in her real life did.

She had friends, at least, the ones Gil hadn't gotten custody of after the divorce. But they were still married. They had children.

A hollow ache filled the empty space where her womb had been. The same one that had plagued her so many times before. When she saw babies. Small children on swings.

Women wiping chocolate stains off of their blouses. And sometimes, it happened for no reason at all. Like now.

"No, reality's one bitch that's pretty hard to ignore," she said.

He chuckled, dark and without humor. "A very true statement. That's why being proactive is important. Sometimes you get problems you didn't make or ask for, but hiding doesn't fix them."

They stopped in front of an elevator and Stavros pushed the button. The gold doors slid open and they stepped inside. The trip down to the lobby was quick, and they breezed through the opulent room quickly, making their way to the front.

There was a limousine waiting for them, black and shiny. Formal. It didn't fit with what she'd seen of Stavros so far. He didn't seem like the type of man who would choose to ride in something so traditional.

He seemed to lurk around the edges of traditional, doing everything a man of his station must do, while keeping one toe firmly over the line of disreputable. It ought to make him obnoxious. It ought to make him less attractive. It didn't.

He opened the door for her and they both slid inside. She sighed, grateful for the air-conditioning. Kyonos was beautiful, but if the breeze from the sea wasn't moving inland it could be hotter than blazes for a girl from North Dakota.

As soon as they settled in and the limo was on the road, she turned to him. "So, why a limo?"

"It's how things are done," he said. He pushed on a panel and it popped open, revealing two bottles of beer on ice. "More or less."

She laughed and held her hand out. "You're about fifteen degrees off unexpected, aren't you?"

He chuckled and handed her a bottle. "Am I?"

"Yes. Hiring a matchmaker to find you a wife and drinking beer in a limo. I'd say you're not exactly what people expect in a prince."

"There are protocols that must be observed, responsibilities that must handled. But there are other things that have a bit more leeway."

"And you take it."

He shrugged. "You have to take hold to the pleasures in life, right?"

"If by pleasures, you mean shoes, then yes."

He laughed and took a bottle opener from a hook on the door and extended his hand, popping the top on the bottle for her. "A true gentleman," she said. "And clearly a professional. Get a lot of practice in college?"

"Like most people."

"Where did you go to school?"

"I did two years in the U.K., two in the U.S."

She nodded. "You would be best suited to a woman who's well traveled, who understands a variety of cultures. Probably someone multilingual."

"Because I'm clearly so cultured?" he asked, raising his bottle. He relaxed his posture, his arm over draped over the back of his seat. There was something so inviting about the pose. The perfect spot for a partner to sit and snuggle against him…

She blinked. "Well, yes, you have to be able to communicate with your spouse. Connect with them on a cerebral level."

"Most of the women I've dated have only connected with me on one level, but it's a level I've found to be very important." The suggestive tone of his voice left no doubt as to just what level he was referring to.

She cleared her throat and tried to banish the heat in her cheeks. For heaven's sake. Talking about sex was normal in her job. It was part of the job, because it was part of relationships. It never made her…blush. She was actually blushing. Really and truly. Like a schoolgirl. Ridiculous.

After enough invasive doctor visits for three lifetimes she thought she'd lost the ability to do that years ago.

"And I consider that important, too," she said, knowing she sounded stiff and a little bit prudish, and she absolutely wasn't either thing, so she had no idea why. "But you will be expected to see each other outside of the bedroom."

"Of course," he said. "But as I said, I have my priorities. Even sexual attraction takes a backseat to a spotless reputation and the ability to produce heirs."

"Right. And how do we establish for certain if she can… produce heirs?"

"Most women can, I assume." He said it with such throwaway carelessness. As though the idea of a woman not being able to have children was almost ridiculous.

She pursed her lips. "And some can't." Why did the subject always make her feel sick? Why did it always make her feel like a failure?

Well, discussing the ability to bear children as an essential trait of a queen, a wife, was never going to be easy, no matter how much peace she imagined she'd made with her lot in life.

"As we get closer to choosing someone, we'll have to undergo a medical screening."

"You'll be required to do the same," she said.

"Will I?"

"Well, yes, I'm not allowing any of the women I might find for you to sleep with you until I establish that you have a clean bill of health."

"You need me to get tested for STDs?"

"Yes. I do. You're planning on having children with the

woman who marries you, which means unprotected sex. And that means a risk to the health of your wife."

"I assume the women will be undergoing the same tests?"

"All of the women who come to me, all of the women and men in my file, are required to submit those test results to me."

"As it happens, I just got tested. Clean. You can have the results if you like."

"I would like them. And I assume you won't be taking on any more sexual partners while we undergo this process?" She felt her cheeks heating again. The topic of sex and Stavros, in the close proximity of the limo, was just a bit too much.

His eyes flickered over her, leaving heat behind. "Naturally not," he said, the words coming slowly. Unconvincingly. "And I haven't had one in quite a while."

"Good. Also, you will not sleep with the women I introduce to you. They know the rules. I don't allow sex between my clients."

"You don't?" he asked, an incredulous laugh in his voice.

"Not until a match is set and I'm not longer involved. Clearly, the relationship can still dissolve, but I'm not a pimp. I'm not prostituting anyone, and I'm not allowing them to prostitute themselves. This is about creating a relationship, a real lasting relationship, not about helping people hook up casually."

"I suppose, running it as a business, you would have to be careful of that," he said.

"Very. When I was starting the business I was really excited, and then I realized what it could quickly turn into if I didn't lay the rules out. Men…well, and women…could use it to find suitable people to…use. And that's not what I want."

"So, you're not a big one for romance, and yet, this is what you choose to do for a living? Why is that?"

She looked out the window, at the crystalline sea and white sand blurring into a wash of color. "It was what I was doing anyway, though not on this level. But after…when I made some changes in life and started my own business, I knew that somehow…I knew relationships could work."

"So you went looking for the formula."

"Yes. And I don't have the only method, though mine has proven highly successful, but I think the way I go about it works. It also helps to have a disinterested party involved who doesn't have their heart in it. That's me. I help people think things through rationally. I set rules so that physical lust doesn't cloud everything else, doesn't create a false euphoria."

"And why don't you apply it to yourself?"

She laughed. "Because. First of all, I can't be my own disinterested party. Second, I don't have the energy or the desire to do it again. I had one big white wedding and I do not intend to do it again."

"Yet you watch other people do it. Get married, I mean."

"Yes. But I find that it…helps. It's restored my faith in humanity a little bit."

The corner of his lip lifted in a sneer. "Was your ex that bad?"

She shook her head slowly. "Sometimes people change, and they change together. Sometimes one person changes. And the other person can't handle it."

It had been her. She'd changed. Her body had changed. And it had altered everything the marriage was built on. Their dreams for the future. It had been too much.

"You're selling the institution so well," he said dryly. He punched the intercom button on the limo divider. "Stop us at Gio's." He let up on the button.

"I'm not trying to sell you the institution. You *have* to get married."

"True."

"And most people who come to me want marriage, or need it for some reason. My personal story, just one of a sad, all too common statistic, will hardly dissuade them. And I'll admit, most of them don't bother to ask about my personal life."

"I find that hard to believe," he said, as the limo slowed and turned onto a narrow road that wound up a hillside.

"Do you?"

"You're interesting. Your clothes for example—interesting. The things that come out of your mouth, also interesting. You beg to have questions asked of you."

"You would be in the minority in that opinion."

"Again, I find it hard to believe."

"I'm very boring. I have a house in North Dakota. I grew up there. Obviously, I don't work with many billionaires, royalty or socialites in North Dakota. I do a lot of work online, and I travel a lot. I'd say my house is empty at least eight months out of the year. I live alone. Can't have a cat because…well, the traveling. So that's me."

"You skipped a lot."

"Did I?"

He leaned in, his head turned to the side. Sort of like how a man looked right before he kissed a woman. If she could even remember back that far, to when she'd experienced anything close to it. "You didn't tell me why you're so prickly."

She leaned in a fraction. "And I don't intend to. Stop flirting with me."

"Am I flirting with you?"

"I think so." If he wasn't that was just too horrifying.

"I can't help it. You're beautiful."

She swallowed. "Look, I know women melt at your feet and all, but I have a job to do, so best you leave me unmelted, okay?"

He leaned back, his lips curving into a smile. "But you're in danger of melting."

She was afraid she might be. "No. Sorry."

He chuckled and settled back in his seat.

The limo stopped in front of a small, whitewashed building that was set into the side of a mountain. The building was tiny, but the deck was expansive, filled with round tables, most occupied by diners. The tables overlooked the beach, with strings of white lights running overhead.

"Ready?" he asked.

She nodded and put her beer in a cupholder. He got out of the car before her and opened her door. "Isn't your driver supposed to do that?" she asked.

He shook his head. "I always open the door when I accompany a woman."

"Another one for your file," she said.

"I'm not sure whether I'm nervous or aroused at the talk of this file. Makes me feel like I'm in trouble, which leads to the same conflicting feelings."

Heat flooded her cheeks, her stomach. "That's inappropriate."

"You're the only one who can make jokes?"

"No...but I didn't make any that were that bad."

"BA? Bedroom Activities?"

"That was serious!" she sputtered as they walked into the restaurant.

"Prince Stavros." A maître d' walked to the door quickly, her willingness to serve the prince obvious, as was the blush staining her cheeks. "I wasn't aware you were coming today."

He winked. "I'm being spontaneous."

"Of course," the woman said. "Your usual table is available. Shall I bring you your usual dinner? For…two?"

Jessica opened her mouth to correct the woman's assumption, but Stavros cut her off.

"That will do nicely. I can show us to my table."

He led the way through the indoor dining area, and heads turned as they passed. Stavros had a sort of effortless charisma that poured from him, touching everyone who saw him. She could imagine, so easily, the kind of woman he would need.

One who could match his ease. His strength. Someone to create the perfect image for Kyonos. Someone to carry on the bloodline and keep it strong.

She swallowed a strange, unexpected lump in her throat.

They exited the dining room through two glass doors that led out to the deck. There were only a few scattered tables out there, each partly shrouded by draping fabric hung from a wooden frame built over the porch.

Stavros held her chair out for her and she sat, looking out at the view of the ocean, because it was much safer than looking at the man sitting across from her. She wasn't sure why. She had meetings with male clients, and very often they were lunch or dinner meetings, in very nice restaurants.

But being with them didn't evoke this same strange faux-date feel that being with Stavros did. It was that darned attraction.

She opened her purse and pulled out her iPad. "So, I know we were going to talk about specific women to have come to your sister's wedding."

"Were we? Now?" He curled his hands into fists on the table, his knuckles turning white. It was hard for her to look away from his hands, from the obvious strain. His face remained passive, easy, but his manner betrayed him.

"Well, no, but I wasn't expecting to see you until tomorrow, so…no. But we can talk about it now. I've had a chance to think about what you've told me and I've been through my system. I also called two of the three women I'm thinking of and if you're agreeable to them, they're willing to come for consideration."

"This is like an old-fashioned marriage mart."

"Well, these sorts of marriages are," she said. Strangely, she felt like comforting him. She didn't know why. "Granted, you're the first actual prince I've worked with. But I've dealt with lesser royals. Billionaires with an interest in preserving their fortunes. Women with family money who wanted an alliance with businessmen who could help them make the most of their assets. People have all kinds of reasons for choosing to go about things this way. Some of these women have money, but no title, while others have a title but are…low on funds."

"Ah. A title, but no money and a need for a husband with wealth."

"Some of them. Though this one…" She pulled up a picture of a smiling blonde. "Victoria Calder. She's English, from a very well-to-do family. She's not titled but she's wealthy. She's been to the best schools. She has her own money and she donates a lot of it to charities. As far as my research has taken me, and it took me to the far and seedy recesses of the internet, her reputation is as spotless as a sacrificial lamb. So if a prominent title isn't important…"

"As long as you think she would be suitable to the position, she can be considered."

"So basically fertile and scandal-free. And able to handle public appearances with grace and poise, of course."

Stavros took the tablet from Jessica's hand and looked at the photo of the woman on the screen. She was beautiful. More than beautiful, really. He couldn't find fault with her features. A small, pert nose, pretty, well-shaped lips, rosy cheeks, pale blue eyes.

Yet she did nothing for him. She didn't stir his blood. She didn't interest him. More than that, just looking at her made his throat feel like it was tightening. The impression of a noose.

He preferred Jessica's face. Her longer nose, fuller lips, cat green eyes that tilted at the corners. And her figure... she was like a pin-up girl.

He wondered, not too briefly, if she favored old-fashioned undergarments to go with her vintage dresses. Stockings and garters.

That caused a surge of blood to pump south of his belt. She was a distraction. A temptation. A welcome one, in many ways.

"Yes." He shouldn't be allowing distraction now. He had to focus on finding his bride.

Though, Ms. Jessica Carter would make an intriguing lover. She was all soft curves and pale skin. But her eyes... they showed a fire he imagined she set free in the bedroom. She was spicy, her tongue always ready to flay the skin cleanly off the bone if necessary.

Just as she'd pronounced his commanding personality a plus in bedroom activities, he imagined her sharp mind and bold tongue would earn her points in her own BA category.

It would be so sweet. So good. And a welcome distraction from the marriage talk.

"Anyway," Jessica continued, pulling him from his fantasy, "she's one I would like to invite to your sister's wedding."

"And she's aware of just what she'll be invited for?"

Jessica nodded. "Yes. All of the women I'm working with have come to me, seeking out husbands that are suitable to their backgrounds and financial level, just the same as you."

"I see. So invariably my future wife will be after a title and wealth—" he looked at the photo of the blonde again "—just as I am."

"Fair is fair. You both know just what you're getting into. No false expectations. Not if I can help it."

"No false expectations? Then can I assume you're including a list of my faults in the file you'll be sending on to the women involved?"

"Only if they make it past a certain point in the process. Discretion," she said.

"Of course." He looked at her face, illuminated and washed gold by the afternoon sun. She was beautiful. Not due to perfection of features, or from the expertly applied makeup, though. Her features were beautiful, and her makeup was expertly done. But it was something more. Something deeper.

She was captivating. Different.

Sexy.

His stomach tightened. "And the first wave of the process begins at my sister's wedding."

"That's right. Is that okay? Or do you feel it will detract from—"

"It's fine," he interrupted. It was strange to think of Evangelina married. To think of her as a woman rather than a little girl. "My sister is in love," he said.

"That's good. Since she's getting married."

He gave her a look. "But you know that's not really how things work around here. Not necessarily."

"True."

"She was meant to marry for the good of Kyonos. She is marrying her bodyguard instead."

"Are you angry about it?" she asked, her eyes meeting his, the glittering green light in them far too perceptive.

"Not in the least. Anger is a completely unproductive

emotion." As were most emotions. He's witnessed it first-
hand. He made sure he didn't have time for them.

"But that leaves only you."

He shrugged. "Doesn't matter. I can do it."

"And your brother…"

"Might as well be dead. He doesn't care for his country. He doesn't care for his family, his people. He might as
well have died with our mother." The words tasted bitter
on his tongue and he wished he had some ouzo to wash it
out with. Bitterness wasn't helpful, either.

As if on command, a waiter appeared with a tray, laden
with food and drinks, and set them down on their table.
Stavros took the drink first, while Jessica picked up a
stuffed grape leaf and turned it in her fingers.

He took a quick hit of the strong alcohol. "I'm happy for
Eva. And her husband does bring a lot to the country in
terms of assets and security. Mak is a billionaire several
times over. She's hardly marrying beneath herself, even if
he isn't royalty."

Beneath Stavros's casual manner, Jessica could sense his
dark mood. He was very good at playing smooth, very good
at coming across as the genial prince. Ready to smile for
a photograph. Never caught scowling by a scandal-hungry
public, who would latch onto the salacious headline de-
claring one grumpy expression proof of some sort of na-
tional crisis.

And yet, she could feel that something wasn't right. That
there was something beneath it.

He was the last man standing. The anchor. How could he
not feel it? Of course he would. His sister had abandoned
her duty for love, his brother had abandoned it for selfish,
personal pleasure. It was only Stavros now.

She felt added pressure. She couldn't imagine that he
didn't.

"Well, we'll find you a royal bride who suits the needs of Kyonos, and you, perfectly," she said, injecting a confidence and enthusiasm into her voice she wasn't sure she felt.

A half smile curved his lips, a shaft of sunlight hitting his face, that single moment displaying the breathtaking quality he possessed to its very best effect.

She certainly felt as if her breath had been taken. Ripped straight from her lungs. Why did he have to be so hot? More to the point, why did she have to suddenly care how hot he was?

She looked back down at her iPad, at the picture of Victoria Calder. And for the first time ever, she felt her stomach curl in with jealousy in connection with a client.

It was the first and last time it would happen. She couldn't afford it. Not financially, and most especially not emotionally.

She'd already had everything drained from her in that department. She would never put herself through it again.

CHAPTER THREE

JESSICA tried not to die of despair as she watched one of her favorite potential brides, Dominique Lanphier, standing by the buffet table looking like a deer in the headlights. She was sort of fidgeting, looking as if she was ready to dart away from the table at a moment's notice and grab Stavros from Corinthia, the petite redhead he was currently engaging in approved conversation with.

This wasn't her best idea. She could see that now. It was just a pity she was realizing it far too late to change anything. Her prospective brides, normally so well-behaved, were a bit giddy over the chance to compete for a prince and all of the good manners that had been bred into them seemed to have been knocked from their heads the moment they'd entered the palace.

Jessica was sweating. Actually sweating. And trying not to look like anything more than a guest. Which, in the grand ballroom, filled to maximum capacity with nearly one thousand people, shouldn't be too hard.

Victoria, her best hope for Stavros, had been unavailable for the wedding, which had forced her to bring in Dominique as a last-minute replacement. Something she was bitterly regretting.

"Just stay there," she whispered, begging Dominique to

go with the program, hoping the other woman would absorb the command from across the room.

It just seemed to be getting hotter in the ballroom now, and she could swear the sweetheart neckline of her flirty cocktail dress was about to slip and go from sexy to burlesque. And that would draw far more attention to herself than she wanted.

She gripped the sides of the bodice and tugged at it slightly. Feeling, for a moment, every inch the unsophisticated North Dakota girl she was on the inside. Feeling her persona start to slip.

No. You are not unsophisticated. You are a businesswoman. You are in a castle. Own your inner princess!

Yes. Inner princess. She was sure she had one of those.

She took a deep breath and felt a bit of her anxiety ease as Stavros checked his watch and disengaged Corinthia right on time. Any longer and there would be speculation. And now, he would go to the buffet and it would be Dominique's turn.

This sort of brief, public meeting, was, in her experience, the perfect way to open. To see people interact in a social situation, to prevent a feeling of enhanced intimacy too quickly.

She had to remind herself of all the reasons it was a good idea now, since she was on the verge of panicking and eating her weight in wedding cake to try and stave off the anxiety. This was what she did. This was her one area of confidence, of expertise. And watching it go very much not according to plan was crazy-making.

The transition went smoothly and she watched Stavros engage Dominique in conversation. So casual it could have been accidental. He was good.

She watched as he leaned in, his body language indicating interest, the smile on his face warm. Genuine. Her throat tightened a bit, and cut off the flow of air entirely when he brushed Dominique's arm with his hand.

Such a brief touch. And yet, it spoke of attraction.

He hadn't touched her. Not more than a handshake. And that brief touch at the restaurant. She shouldn't have a list of the times his skin had made contact with hers. It shouldn't matter that he was touching someone else.

It shouldn't matter. It didn't. She was here to try and match him with one of these women. This choking jealousy had no place in it. Jealousy was an awful emotion. Consuming. It brought out the worst in people, in her particularly.

When she'd found out Gil was getting married again. When she'd found out his wife was pregnant.

A prickle of shame spread from her scalp through her body.

She shouldn't be jealous of Gil's wife. Of her ability to give birth. It was small and petty. If he couldn't find happiness with her, he should be free to find it with someone else.

The thing that sucked was that he'd found the happiness she'd wanted. He'd been able to move on and get all of the hopes and dreams they'd built their marriage on. He'd been able to leave her.

She couldn't leave herself.

Her body was her body. Her limitations wouldn't change with a new partner. Moving on for her meant something very different than it had for her ex. Moving on meant rebuilding, finding new dreams. She was happy. She had a successful business. She was financially solvent and she was matchmaking for a prince, for heaven's sake.

A prince she should have no feelings for at all. And certainly not any kind of longing type feelings.

Crazy was what it was. Crazy.

Stavros's time with Dominique closed and he made a

polite exit, not lingering for a moment longer. Which suggested he couldn't have gotten too lost in her eyes or anything.

She should not feel satisfied by that.

She felt her stomach free-fall when Stavros changed course suddenly and started walking toward her. His movements easy, his manner approachable. And several people did approach him. He managed to make everyone feel he'd expended attention on them without actually taking much time, barely halting his movement. Every so often, his dark eyes would land on her, leaving her in no doubt that she was his destination.

And, well, he was a prince, and he was a client. So she wasn't going to dodge him.

She stood, rooted to the spot, until Stavros stopped in front of her. "I'd love a word with you in private," he said.

She looked around. "As long as we don't draw attention. I'm hardly the most recognizable face in the world but…"

"Come," he said. Taking her hand and striding toward the ballroom's exit, his gait much more purposeful than it had been a moment ago.

She snagged a glass of champagne off of a passing waiter's tray and followed him out. "Wait. I'm in heels," she said, taking quick, tottering steps out into the corridor. She flashed a passing guest a smile and tried to match Stavros's pace. "Hey, Tarzan. Me not Jane. You no drag me out by the hair."

He ignored her, continuing to walk down the hall until he came to an ornate wood door that she recognized as the entrance to his office. She never would have found it by herself. Not in the maze of halls the Kyonosian palace boasted. He released her hand, entered in a code and pushed the door open. "Come in," he said.

She shot him a look and walked into the room, wiping

her hand on the tulle skirt of her gown, trying to get rid of the heated feeling that his touch had left behind. She crossed her arms beneath her breasts, pushed her cleavage up into prominence, then thought better of it when she realized just how prominent it was.

She put her hands on her hips. "What's up?"

"None of them were acceptable," he said.

"None?"

"No."

"But...but..." she sputtered. "What about Dominique? You touched her arm."

He shrugged. "I know how to flirt."

"Well, yeah, I know, I yelled at you for it a while back. But why flirt if you aren't going to follow up?"

He frowned. "Did you just imply that I am a...tease?"

"Yeah. A marriage tease. Why feign interest if you don't feel any?"

"I'm not seeking to hurt anyone's feelings," he said dryly. "I could hardly stand there and act bored. And anyway, that begs the question why you would send me such dull women."

"Dull? Dominique is a beauty queen, Corinthia is a doctor, for heaven's sake, and Samantha..."

"Had the most annoying laugh."

"All right. Yes, her laugh is kind of annoying. But it's sort of endearing."

"No. It's not."

"You're being unkind."

"Maybe. But I don't have forever to find a wife, and you were supposed to be the best."

"I am," she said. "I can find you a wife. Anyway, I didn't think your personal preferences came into it."

"I don't want to be...irritated into an early grave by a woman who laughs at all my jokes, even when they aren't funny, or by one who can't seem to make conversation about anything other than the weather."

"That's called small talk. It's how people get to know each other," she said.

"Boring." He waved a hand as if dismissing the concept. "Talk about world events. Something other than the 'balmy evening.'"

"So marriage is more to you than you said. Glad to hear it."

"I am not glad that you presented me with unacceptable candidates. This is not about…meaning, or emotions. This is about… I have to be able to stand the woman I marry."

"You really are being ridiculous. They weren't unacceptable. What's the problem? You didn't find them attractive?"

"They were attractive. But I was not attracted *to* any of them."

"You say that like it's my fault."

"It is," he said, whirling around to face her. His dark gaze slid down to her breasts and her own followed.

She looked back up at him. "Elaborate," she said, teeth gritted.

"You expect that you can show up in that dress, and I can focus on other women?"

"What's wrong with my dress?" She gripped the full, tulle skirt reflexively.

"Other than the fact that you're showing off much more of your breasts than any straight man could be expected to ignore? It also shows your legs. This was a formal wedding. Every other woman, including the ones I was speaking to, had on long gowns. You…you…"

"This dress comes to my knees. And I didn't realize you were a fourteen-year-old boy masquerading as a prince."

The insult rolled off her tongue, because what he was saying felt far too good. She wanted to turn it over in her mind, to savor it. To pretend that it was for her and that it mattered. To bask in being seen as pretty instead of broken.

The thought made her so annoyed with herself she wanted to scream.

He took a step toward her, and she sucked in a breath, holding her ground. He leaned in, his face close to hers, dark eyes intense. "I can assure you, I am not a boy."

She swallowed, fought the urge to put her hand on his cheek and see if the faint, dark shadow there was rough yet. "I believe it."

"Then do not test me." His eyes held hers, her heart threatening to beat clean through her chest. She pulled away, her breathing shallow.

Stavros turned away from her. She stood in the middle of his office as he paced, each movement languid and deadly. Her heart was pounding, her body shaking. She'd known that he couldn't possibly be so easy, so relaxed. Beneath that charm lurked the soul of a predator. The deadliest sort, because he knew how to portray an air of complete and utter harmlessness.

Stavros Drakos was anything but harmless. How had she not seen it? How had she assumed he was all flirtation and ease?

And had he…had he really just confessed to finding her cleavage distracting? She looked down again and felt a small flush of pride creep into her cheeks. It had been a long time since she'd been able to feel anything overly positive in connection with her body.

It was nice to have a man look at her and simply see a woman.

It might be a facade, a trick, but it didn't really matter. Stavros would never have to get closer. Would never have to know the truth, or deal with the fallout of it.

But that didn't mean she wouldn't enjoy it. Just for a moment.

"I wasn't intending to," she said.

He stopped moving. "You cannot be ignorant of how you look. You outshone the bride."

She couldn't believe that. Not seriously. Princess Evangelina was a great beauty. Olive skin, long dark hair and a slender figure. In her wedding gown, she was unsurpassable. Plus, the princess was only twenty-one. She didn't have the years Jessica had on her body. Didn't have the scars.

"I doubt that," she said.

"My eyes were on you most of the time."

Heat rushed up her neck and into her face, then spread down over her breasts. "We should not be having this conversation."

"We should. Because if you're going to be present at all of my meetings with potential fiancées, you need to dress more suitably."

"I will dress how I please, Prince Stavros," she said, feeling her hackles rise. She really didn't do backed into a corner well, and, at the moment, she felt backed into a corner.

Stavros felt his pulse pounding in his neck, all of his blood rushing south of his belt. He'd been fighting to urge to go and pull Jessica into his arms and kiss her lips, kiss the swells of her breasts where they rose up over that gown. That ridiculous gown that made her look like every man's midnight fantasy.

He'd tried to focus on the women, the bridal candidates. But they'd seemed…insipid. Young. They hadn't interested him. They certainly hadn't stirred his body. Not in the way Jessica did. And that was not part of tonight's plan.

But when she'd walked into the ballroom tonight, it was as though a switch had flipped inside of him.

Lust had ignited in him like fire, the need to see her curves, those gorgeous curves, without a dress covering them. It made him want to press her against the wall and push all that frilly netting aside. To make her scream with the kind of desire that seemed to be actively trying to eat him alive every time she was around.

He was better than this. He mastered his desires. He directed them where he wanted, when he wanted to express them.

"Has anyone ever told you that you are very stubborn?" he growled.

"It's probably been said to me as many times as it's been said to you. Actually, I imagine I've heard it more, since people probably don't stand up to you very often."

That much was true. But she stood up to him, and she did it without compunction. Yes, she had a reputation for being this bullheaded, but he hadn't expected she would truly treat him in the same way she did every other client.

His expectation had been wrong.

"Fair enough then," he said. "But I do expect you to do as I ask."

"Then I expect you might find yourself disappointed."

"You are supposed to be working for me," he said, not sure where this urge to push her was coming from. But that was what he was doing. Pushing her. Daring her.

"If that's how you feel, you can hunt for your own wife. But we both know you don't want that."

"I'm not sure I want this." The closest he'd ever come to voicing the truth to anyone.

"But you will." She was so certain. And she was right. Emotion had no place in this. It had no place in him.

He crossed his arms. "You have other candidates?"

"You still haven't met Victoria. And there are others."

She shifted and so did her cleavage. A flame licked at his body, igniting desire. Arousal.

"We can discuss it further later. Shall we go back to the wedding?"

"Yes."

She pursed her lips and raised an eyebrow. "And will you be civilized?"

A loaded question, and one he was certain applied to more than just tonight. An answer he wasn't certain of. "I suppose you'll have to take your chances. Are you willing to do that?"

He extended his arm and she didn't move for a beat. Then she took a step to him and looped her arm through his. "You don't worry me too much, Stavros."

He felt a kick in his gut, a purely masculine part of himself taking her words as a challenge. He stopped, turning to face her. Her green eyes widened, lips parting.

"You trust me?" he asked, his heart thundering.

Her eyes drifted to his mouth before raising up to meet his. "Yes."

"Ah, but, Ms. Carter, I'm not certain I trust myself. You certainly shouldn't be putting any trust in me."

It was nothing. Just a little lust. Nothing deeper than any other attraction he'd felt. It was a direct result of his long bout of celibacy. He would meet more women. Find the one he was supposed to marry, and then he could focus all of his desire on her.

But *Theos* help him if he could think of marriage without feeling like he was choking. The attraction to Jessica at least made him feel...well, he could breathe.

"I'm going to be in Greece for the next few weeks and I want you to arrange my meetings with prospective brides there. I have business to attend to." Flexible business, but he needed to get out of Kyonos. Now.

Jessica blinked. "I...I can do that. But I have other clients and I..."

"Not right now you don't. I need you to put everything else on hold. I need you with me, organizing meetings and whatever else I might need so we can simply get this done."

"What will people think if we just up and go to Greece the day after your sister's wedding?"

"Perhaps that we're embarking on a wild affair?" The idea made his body harden. The idea certainly had merit. Merit he might have to seriously consider. Just the idea of lowering her dress, revealing those luscious breasts...

She laughed. "Oh, I doubt that. More than likely they'll wonder if you're looking for a Greek wife."

"I'm not opposed." Not any more opposed than he was to the whole idea.

"I guess it doesn't matter if we operate from Greece or Kyonos."

"Good. Then we'll leave for Greece first thing tomorrow." He opened his office door and held it for her. Tomorrow he would get out of Kyonos, get his head on straight.

For now, he was determined to go back to the reception and enjoy the happiest day of his sister's life.

CHAPTER FOUR

What did one wear on a private jet headed to Greece? With a prince as cabin-mate. That last part was important.

That had been the first question in her mind that morning, and it was still plaguing her even as she boarded the private jet, decked out in a yellow halter-top sundress and a matching wide-brimmed hat.

Because seriously, dwelling on anything more important than that might make her head explode. And she didn't want to risk it. Aside from the fact that the interior was far too swanky to chance getting brain matter on it, she had too much work to do and she couldn't function without said organ.

Stavros was already on the plane, lounging in one of the spacious leather seats, hands behind his head. It was like his go-to mess-with-her-composure position. Exposed bulge at the apex of his thighs? Check. Hard, muscular chest on display? Check. Washboard abs on show? Double check.

He was going to drive her insane.

And what would you do about it? Even if you could act on your attraction to him?

Nothing. The answer was an absolutely nothing, because while attraction, flirtation and sexual desire were all fine and fun, going any further than that would only result in pain. Emotional pain if not physical pain.

Probably both.

"Good morning," she said.

He stood, his posture straight as she moved into the cabin and sat down in a chair that was positioned as far from his as was polite. He didn't sit until she had settled herself.

"I like that," she said. "Very chivalrous."

"Etiquette is, of course, important for a prince to learn," he said, humor lacing his tone.

"It's a dying art form these days, trust me. With both men and women."

"I imagine you would have a greater insight into that than most." He buckled his seat belt and she followed suit as the plane readied for take-off.

"Probably. I deal with people on a pretty regular basis. And I have to ask a lot of…intimate questions. But people also tend to be on their best behavior when they're looking for a relationship, or just beginning one. So I see a lot of the polished squeaky clean veneer, too."

He nodded. "I suppose I do, too."

"I'll bet not many people let loose in front of royalty."

"You don't seem that bothered by my position."

The plane started down the runway and a bubble of excitement burst in her stomach. It had taken a while, but she liked flying now. She liked how free it made her feel. If she wasn't happy where she was, she could hop a plane and escape for a while.

It was liberating; providing some of the few real moments of freedom she felt. It was superhuman to fly, and it took her mind off the fact that she really was just human. With all kinds of shortcomings.

"Well, unlike my clients, I don't see the point in hiding who I am." Lies. She absolutely hid who she was. Behind a suit of armor that was a lot tougher than she was. But what was the point of armor if you admitted you had it on?

"Really?"

"Really."

"I don't believe you," he said, his dark eyes far too perceptive for her liking.

What was he? A mind reader? "Why is that?"

"Because you have secrets. You won't tell me why you're prickly."

She bit the inside of her cheek. "I told you not to flirt with me."

"You tell me that when I start to get close to things you don't want to talk about," he said, leaning over slightly. He was still across the aisle from her, but she felt the move. Felt the increased closeness.

She shifted the opposite direction. "Having secrets is normal. I imagine you have them."

"Not one. Every detail of my life is published in the archives and kept in my father's office. My more public exploits are in the news, in tabloids, on royalty stalker websites."

"So that's it then, you're an open book?"

"I have nothing to hide. More to the point, I can't have anything to hide. If I did, it would be put out in the public eye. I'm a public commodity," he ground out, a bitterness tingeing his words. "I exercise discretion in certain areas of my life, naturally. I don't announce when I take a lover, for example, though all tabloids will imply it. You, on the other hand—you have secrets."

"You think you have me figured out?"

A smile curved his lips. Wicked. Dangerous. "No. Not at all."

"Well, that's good. I would hate to be thought of as predictable."

"You aren't predictable in the least. Not down to what you'll wear on a given day," he said, his eyes on her hat.

"That makes you interesting. It makes me wonder." His eyes met hers and she felt a jolt in her system. "It makes me want to discover all of your secrets."

His made goose bumps break out on her arms. Low and husky, with the kind of accent usually only found in her late-night fantasies. And his eyes...dark and rich, like chocolate. A bitter, intense sort of chocolate.

Her favorite.

She swallowed and tried to slow the beating of her heart. "I live in North Dakota when I'm not traveling, as you already know. I don't own pets. I like clothes. And I do a really dorky celebration dance when I beat my own high scores on computer games." She tried to smile. "Open book."

"I would like to see the dance. But I also don't believe you."

"I do the dance. But I won't do it for you."

"No, I believe you do it." His eyes locked with hers, the perception in them, the sudden seriousness, unnerving her. "I just don't believe you're an open book."

"And I can't believe you care. You don't have time to worry about me or my idiosyncrasies, Prince Stavros, you have a wife to find."

"No, *you* have a wife to find. Deliver her to me when you do."

She laughed, trying to dispel the tension. "That's the plan. Although, I have to do a bit more than deliver. You have to agree with my selection."

"I admit I liked the look of...Victoria, was that her name?"

"Um...yes." She bent down and picked her purse up, hunting for her iPad.

"It's fine. You don't need to get her picture out. I remember."

Was that jealousy? That hot, burning sensation in her stomach? Yes. It very likely was. Ridiculous. She wanted him to like Victoria. Victoria was a fabulous candidate. "Victoria would probably like to meet you here in Greece. She was disappointed that work conflicted with the wedding."

"What happened to your speed-dating idea?"

"I'll get a couple of other girls out as well, just to keep the pressure off. But if I—and by I, I mean you—fly them to Greece they deserve more than fifteen minutes of your time."

"Agreed."

"When will you have time?" She looked back down at her bag.

"Get it out if you have to," he said, his tone grudging.

She leaned down and took her tablet out of her purse and opened the flap on the cover. She opened up the calendar and sat poised with her finger at the ready.

"In the evenings. Dinner dates will do."

She typed in a quick note. "Would you like to see photographs of the other women I'll be asking?"

"Not especially."

She let out an exasperated breath. "If I don't show them to you, you'll only accuse me of picking women who aren't attractive again."

"You can't hear a laugh in a picture. And that laugh was unforgivable."

The look she shot him would have been fatal to a lesser man. "You really are being unkind about the laugh."

"She sounded like a nervous mouse. And she even lifted her hands up and wiggled her fingers. Like she was waiting for cheese."

Jessica tried, and failed to suppress a laugh. "That… you…well."

"I'm right."

"You're mean!"

"I'm not mean. It's one of those things that would eat at me. Day in and day out until one day I divorced her over her laugh and that would be a much bigger unkindness than just not pursuing things from the get go."

She expelled a breath. "Fine. I won't push the laugh issue again. You're entitled to your judgmental opinion."

"I am," he said, lowering his hands so that they were gripping the armrests on his chair. He had such big hands. Very big. Oh…dear. What was her problem?

She lowered her head and focused on her computer. "Anyway, I was thinking of asking Cherry Carlisle and Amy Sutton over." She looked at Stavros, who was affecting a bored expression and staring out the window. "Cherry is a brunette. Amy is a redhead. And Victoria's a blonde." He kept his gaze off of her. "It's actually pretty good because it's like the setup to your own, personal joke. A blonde, a brunette and a redhead go to Greece."

He looked at her, the corners of his mouth tipped upward. "To marry the prince. You really are selling this well."

"I try. Once we land in Greece I'll coordinate with them and hopefully we can get them there ASAP."

"You like speaking in acronyms, don't you?"

She shrugged. "It's faster."

"Speaking of, by my very fast math, you'll be involving six women in this so far. And while I'm under no illusion that we'll keep the press out of this entirely, I wonder what might happen if one of them ends up feeling…jilted."

"Oh, they've signed a gag order."

"A gag order?"

"I take my business very seriously and yes, this is tabloid bait. Serious, serious tabloid bait. And I have no interest in feeding you, or me, to the wolves. So I've taken pretty big precautions."

He leaned forward, his interest obviously piqued now. "And what are the consequences if they break the gag order?"

"Their firstborn child. All right, not quite but there are some monetary fees."

"You are quite deceptive, Ms. Carter."

"Am I?" she asked, leaning back in her chair and crossing her arms beneath her breasts.

"Yes. You seem so sunny. Soft," he said, his dark eyes settling on her breasts. "And yet…you are cynical. More so even than I am, I think. Which is really quite something."

She swallowed and angled her face away from him. She could still feel him looking at her. "Call it cynical if you like, I call it realism. Human nature is what human nature is. No matter how much someone thinks they love you, if being with you starts to conflict with their ultimate goals… well, it won't take much for them to start believing that they don't love you anymore. That's why I work to find people who have united goals and interests. Things that are concrete. Much more concrete than love. Whatever that is. I'm a realist, that's all."

"Cynic. Realist. Whatever the case, you certainly aren't soft."

She shook her head. "No. Being soft hurts too much."

She had no idea why she was telling him so much. What was inspiring her to give away any of her tightly guarded self to this man. She only knew that it was easier to talk around him than to hold it in. That was new. Strange.

She'd always found it easier to just keep it all stuffed inside. Locked behind a wall of iron, defended by her sharp wit. Easier to have an off-the-cuff, half-serious response to everything than to let someone see her true self.

And yet, with Stavros, she had shared.

So pointless and silly. Irritating even, because there was no reason for her to choose him as a confidante. No reason at all. She didn't have a confidante. She didn't need one.

So stop it, already.

"You're right about that," he said, his voice different now. Serious. Lacking that mischief that was usually present. "Emotion…it can eat you alive. Steal every good intention. Every concept of responsibility. We'll be staying in my private villa," he said, changing the subject neatly. And she was grateful.

"We? As in…the two of us?"

"What did you imagine might happen, Jessica?" he asked. Her ears pricked and her heart stuttered at the use of her first name. It felt…intimate.

"I thought maybe we'd stay in a hotel and I'd have my own room." Perhaps a floor or twelve away from his.

"I prefer not to stay in hotels, if I can help it, and you may reserve your comments on the irony of that."

She arched an eyebrow. "How did you know I had a comment ready?"

"You always have a comment ready."

"True," she agreed.

"The villa is big. You won't have to run into me at all, unless it's work-related. If you don't want to, that is."

His voice dropped a step when he said that last part, his words a husky invitation that her body was aching to respond to.

"Why…why would I want to?" she asked, her voice a bit shaky.

"You're the only one who can answer that," he said.

She knew what her answer would be. And it would be completely inappropriate. "Well. I won't. Come looking for you, that is. For anything besides work."

He nodded slowly and leaned back in his seat. "Probably a wise decision."

Probably. And she shouldn't regret making it. But she did.

CHAPTER FIVE

THE villa was everything a prince's Grecian villa should be. Windows that stretched from floor to ceiling and ran the length of the room, offering views of the Aegean that were incomparable. Everything was washed in white and blue, reflecting the pale sun and glittering sea.

"You have a room on the second floor. Ocean view," he said.

"Are there any non-ocean views available?" she asked.

"Not many. But I like to be near the sea. The product of my island upbringing, I would imagine. I used to..." A strange expression crossed his face. "I used to like watching the ships come into harbor. Or sail out to sea." He cleared his throat. "Until I became a teenager, and just enjoyed watching women walk around in bikini bottoms. Either way, I've always liked the beach."

"North Dakota's not by the ocean. It's landlocked."

"I know. And the idea of it makes me feel claustrophobic. How do you stand it?"

"I leave. A lot." Her hometown made her feel claustrophobic more often than not, in truth. Especially since she always ran the risk of seeing Gil and Sarah if she went grocery shopping. And now it was Gil and Sarah and Aiden.

Suddenly the fresh ocean air seemed too briny, too harsh. Her throat tightened against it.

"That's one solution," he said.

"A temporary one."

"Why not make it permanent?"

Because then she really would have to let go. "I own a house. It's nice. I have…petunias."

"And I have bougainvillea. There are flowers everywhere."

"But they're my flowers." And it was the place she could go and rehash where her dreams had started. And where they had ended.

No. Not ended. Changed. She was just hunting for some new ones now. Well, that was total garbage. She had a bunch of new ones. She was successful. She had awesome shoes. She helped people find…well, lasting marriage if not love.

"You could transplant them."

She sighed. "Oh, come on, Stavros, they're only petunias."

He laughed, the sound rich and genuine, catching her off guard. "Perhaps find me a woman *you* wouldn't mind spending time with."

His suggestion caught her off guard more than his laughter. "What do you mean by that?"

"You're funny. Quick. I imagine you don't hang out with people who bore you."

"I don't hang out with much of anyone these days, outside of a working relationship, but you're right, I don't."

"So, find me someone you would be amused by. Someone who has better things to talk about than the weather."

"The weather here is lovely," she said, unable to resist.

"Things like that," he said, amusement lacing his tone. "Find a woman who does things like that."

"So someone who's like me, but not me."

"Exactly."

He was teasing. And even if he weren't, there was no

way she could be suitable. She wasn't sweet and demure. She didn't know how to do a royal wave. And she wasn't fertile. Not even maybe.

The only requirement she met was being a woman, a broken one. And that just wasn't enough.

Still, when she looked at her ex-husband's curvy, blonde new wife, she felt like he had gone and done that same thing. A woman who was her, but not her. He'd found a replacement model with a working, intact uterus.

It was something that still burned no matter how hard she tried to pretend it didn't. She didn't love Gil anymore. She didn't want him back. But the way it had all gone down... that was the really hard thing to deal with.

That was the part she had to process. So she just had to move forward. Inch by inch, day by day. Breath by breath.

Some days were more successful than others.

"Charming," she said, turning and heading toward the staircase.

"Jessica." Stavros caught her arm and turned her to face him, his dark eye intense. "I'm sorry. That came out... It was a bad joke."

She shrugged and tried to pull away from him. Away from his touch. His heat. "It's nothing. I'm just tired. I'll think about what we talked about today and I'll get back to you, okay?"

He released his hold on her, her skin still burning where his flesh had touched hers. Scorched hers. How long had it been since someone had touched her? And by touch, she didn't mean handshakes. Didn't mean brushes of fingers, or even a proprietary male hand on her back as she was guided into a building.

Really touched her. Personal. Caring, almost.

It had been so long. Even longer since she'd felt a real connection with someone. That was actually worse than not being touched. Being touched, being skin-to-skin with someone, and knowing that there was no connection at all.

This wasn't like that. She didn't want to crave it. She'd let go of those desires and had done her very best to replace them with new ones. He was ruining it.

Reflexively, she brushed her fingers over the spot where his had rested. "It's nothing. I'm fine."

"You don't look fine."

"Stavros, I'm fine," she said, finding it easier to use his first name now. Here in the villa and not in the palace. "I'm not vying for the position of wife to the future king of Kyonos, remember? I'm helping you find her. And I will. Promise."

"Have dinner with me," he said.

"Where?"

"Here, at the villa."

The thought of it made her stomach feel all fluttery. It made her palms sweaty, too. She was seriously out of practice when it came to dealing with men. Except she wasn't, not really, she just never got asked to have dinner with them in a way that went beyond business.

And you think this is more than business?

No. Of course it wasn't. She was here, in the villa, and he was being hospitable to someone who was working to find him a wife. And she was not that wife.

She didn't want to be anyway. Not even tempted.

The only reason she'd forgotten, for a moment, that his invitation wasn't meant to be an intimate one, was because he'd touched her arm. It had caused a momentary short circuit but she was back now.

"That would be lovely. We can discuss some women who might have more advanced conversation skills…"

"Leave your computer in your room."

"B-but…"

"Come on, Jessica, I think we can have a conversation without your piece of technical equipment between us."

Did he? Because she didn't think so. She wasn't sure what she would do with her hands. Or what she would look at when she started to melt into those dark chocolate eyes of his and she needed a reprieve.

"Of course. I don't have a problem with that. None at all."

"Good. See you in a couple of hours. That will give you enough time to unpack and freshen up?"

She frowned and touched her hair. Freshen up? Did she need it?

"Not everything I say is a commentary on you. Or me finding you lacking in some way," he said, his tone sardonic.

"Pfft. Of course not," she said, dropping her hand to her side. "And not everything I do is connected to something you say making me feel like I'm lacking in some way."

One dark eyebrow arched upward. "Touché."

"Oh…which way to my room?"

"Pick any room you want. Top of the stairs and turn left. I'm to the right."

Then she would be picking the room at the very, very far end of the hall. Left as left could be. "Great. Thanks. See you down here at seven?"

He cocked his head to the side, that charming, easy grin curving his lips. "Sounds good to me. I'll have your bags sent up soon."

"All right. See you at dinner."

She turned and started up the stairs, the marble clicking beneath her heels.

She wasn't going to change her dress before dinner. Because that would mean she was treating it like it was special. Like a date.

No. She definitely wasn't changing her dress.

* * *

She'd changed her dress. That was the first thing he noticed when Jessica descended the stairs and stepped into the living area.

She'd traded in the cheery, yellow, low-cut halter-top dress for a slinky, red, low-cut dress, belted at her tiny waist. The skirt hugged her rounded hips and fell just to her knee, showing those shapely, sexy calves that he was starting to fixate on.

Not as much as he was fixated on the creamy swells of her breasts. But close.

"Hello," she said. Her posture was stiff, her elegant neck stretched up as tall and tight as possible. Her cherry-painted lips were thinned. Which was a waste in his mind. If a woman was going to wear red lipstick she should pout a little. Especially this woman.

But it wasn't the sexual feelings she stirred in him that disturbed him. It was the way she'd looked at him earlier… sad, hurt. And how he'd wanted to drop everything, the wall he put between himself and everyone he interacted with, to comfort her.

That feeling, that desire for a true connection, was foreign to him. And if not entirely foreign, connected to the distant past. Back when he'd believed he had a different future ahead of him. Back before he'd realized the importance of erasing any feeling that could root itself inside of him too deeply.

That might control him. Weaken him. As emotion had weakened his father.

"Good evening," he said, inclining his head. "Have you started settling in?"

"Yes. It's lovely here." The corners of her lips turned up slightly. "Very…balmy."

The small talk was too crisp. Too bland. And Jessica Carter was neither of those things. What she was, was prickly as a porcupine and likely making inane talk to ir-ritate him. It shouldn't. With women he was all about con-necting on a surface level. With people in general. Why did he want more from her?

Why did she make him want more for himself?

Talking to that woman with the mouse laugh…it had been grating. Insufferable. Just the thought of being shack-led to her for the rest of his life… It had seemed personal in a way it hadn't before. Whether that was due to Jessica or the wedding being more of a reality, he didn't know.

"Tell me about your dress," he said, because he knew it would catch her off guard. It would also redirect his thoughts to her delicious figure, and that was acceptable. The rest, the feeling, was not.

She blinked rapidly a few times. "My dress?"

He started to walk toward the terrace, where dinner was waiting for them. "Yes, your dress. What's the story behind it? A woman who makes clothing her hobby surely has a story for each item."

"Yes. Well, but I didn't think you would be interested." She was walking behind him, trying to keep pace in her spiky black heels.

He hadn't thought he would be interested, either. Strangely, he was. "I live to surprise." He paused at the table and pulled her chair out. "Sit. And tell me."

She arched one well-shaped brow. "I don't respond to one-word commands."

Heat fired through his veins, pooling in his stomach. His answering remark came easily. And it was welcome as it served to mask the intense need that gripped him. "I'll bet there are a few one-word commands I could get you to respond to."

She sat quickly and picked up the glass of white wine that was waiting for her, taking a long drink before setting it down and saying, far too brightly, "I found this dress at a charity shop."

He rounded the table and sat across from her, keeping the chair pushed out a bit. He didn't trust himself to get too close. And clearly, Jessica didn't, either. Her change of topic had been about as clumsy and obvious as they came.

She'd picked up the meaning of his words. And he'd driven her to drink. That was an ego boost.

"Go on," he said.

"It's from the late forties or early fifties. Sort of business attire."

"That was business attire?" It was a wonder any work got done.

"Clothing then was so feminine. It didn't have to be obvious to be sexy, and it didn't have to be boxy to be respectable. That's one reason I like it."

It was certainly that. But then, Jessica would look feminine in a man's suit. She had curves that simply couldn't be ignored or concealed.

"It suits you," he said.

"I'm glad you think so. You looked at me like I had two heads the first couple of days we were together."

"Did I?"

"Yes."

"I hope you like fish," he said, indicating the plate of food. He always opted for simple when he was at the villa. Something from the sea, vegetables from the garden on the property and a basket of bread and olive oil. He had all the formal he could handle in Kyonos. Ceremony and heavy custom, though he'd been born into it, had never seemed to fit him. Just one reason he was always skirting the edge of respectability.

That and a desire—no, a need—to control something about his life.

"I do," she said. "I didn't always, but as we've discussed, my home state is landlocked, so seafood wasn't that fresh. And fish out of the river just tastes like a river and it's not a good experience. Not for me, anyway. Traveling has expanded my horizons in a lot of ways."

"Was your husband from North Dakota?"

A crease appeared between her eyebrows. "Yes."

"Is that why you aren't with him anymore?"

Her mouth dropped open. "No. What's that supposed to mean?"

"Nothing," he said. But he had wondered, when she spoke of travel, of not spending time at her home, if her ambitions had grown bigger than the life of a housewife.

"Are you asking if I traded my husband in for—" she waved her fork over her plate "—for fresh seafood?"

"Not in so many words."

"Well, I didn't." She released a heavy breath. "If only it were that simple."

"It's not simple?"

"It is now," she said, stabbing at the white flesh of the fish on her plate. "Because we're divorced, and he's my *ex*-husband, not my husband. So whatever happened between us doesn't really matter. That's the beauty of divorce."

An unfamiliar twinge of guilt stabbed at him. "You wouldn't be the first person to run from an unhappy situation. To try and find peace somewhere else." He thought of Xander when he spoke those words. Xander, who had been so miserable. Who had been blamed for the death of their mother. By their father, by their people. And sadly, in the end, by Stavros himself.

"I'm the one who left, if that's what you want to know," she said, her voice cold.

His stomach tightened. She'd walked away. He didn't know the story, he didn't know her pain. But still, it was so easy for him to judge her. It was his gut reaction. Because he knew what happened when people walked away just because it was too hard.

"Did he mistreat you?" Stavros asked.

She met his gaze, her green eyes glittering. "That's a loaded question."

"Seems simple to me."

"All right, I think he was an ass, but then, I'm his ex-wife." She looked down. "Really? He's a moral paragon. You know, he could have taken a lot of money from me. I was the main breadwinner. And he didn't. He didn't want it. He just wanted to be free of me. He took the out I gave him and ran." She pushed her plate back. "I'm not hungry." She stood and put her napkin on the table. "Thanks, but I'm going to go to bed now." She turned and walked away, her shoulders stiff.

Stavros wanted to go after her. To grab her arm like he'd done earlier. To soothe her. With a touch. A kiss.

He sucked in long breath, trying to ease the tightness in his chest. To kiss those ruby lips…they would be so soft.

He wanted to offer comfort. To hold her in his arms.

He couldn't do any of those things.

So he let her go, while his body bitterly regretted every step she took away from him.

Jessica flopped onto the bed and growled fiercely into the empty room. "Way to spill your guts there, Jess," she scolded herself.

Why had she told him that? Any of that. Yes, he'd pushed the subject of Gil. And yes, it had gotten her hackles up because she didn't want any judgment from him about her marriage.

But it was hard to talk about it without talking about everything. About the reason things had crumbled. About the pain, the embarrassment. About the bitterness and disappointment laced into every word. About how going to bed at night had been something she'd dreaded. To have to share a bed with someone, maybe even make love with someone, when they were distant at best, disdainful at worst.

About how in the end she'd had to face the hardest, scariest thing she'd ever endured on her own. About how her husband had let her have major surgery without his support, without him there. She'd had to just lie by herself in a hospital bed. Her body had hurt so bad, and her heart had been crumbling into pieces, the victory over her chronic condition costing her her dearest dreams.

And that was when she'd called a lawyer. She hated that. That he'd made her do that. She honestly believed if she hadn't he would have stayed. Would have punished her by making her live with a man who had grown to hate her.

She closed her eyes and blocked out the memory. As much as she could, she just tried to pretend those moments were a part of someone else's life. Sometimes it worked. Just not right now.

She stood up and started pacing the length of the room. She was pathetic. And pitiful. And where was her armor when she needed it?

There was a knock on the door and she paused midstride. "Yes?" she asked.

"It's me."

The very masculine voice was unmistakable. As was the shiver of excitement that raced through her.

She turned and flung the door open, putting her hand on her hip and shifting her weight so that her hip stuck out, exaggerating the roundness of her curves. "What?"

He only looked at her, his dark eyes glittering. A muscle in his jaw ticked, his shoulders flexed.

They stood for a moment and simply looked at each other.

Then Stavros moved, quickly, decisively, and pulled her up against the hard wall of his chest. He dipped his head and his lips met hers. Hot. Hungry.

So good.

She clung to the door with one hand, her other hand extended next to her, balled into a fist as Stavros kissed her, his hands roaming over her back, his tongue tracing the outline of her lips. And when it dipped inside, slid against her tongue, that was when she released her hold on the door and locked her arms around his neck, forking her fingers through his hair.

He turned her so that her back was against the door frame, his hands moving to her waist.

Oh, yes, she wanted this. All of it. More.

She moved her hands to his shoulders, let them roam over his back. He was hot and strong, his muscles shifting beneath her fingertips. His shirt felt too thick, scratchy on her skin. She wanted to pull it off of him. She arched against him, her breasts pressing against his chest, and she became aware of just how present her dress was. How much of an impediment it was.

They needed to get rid of their clothes.

She moved her hands around to his chest, toyed with the first button on his dress shirt. He growled, a masculine, feral sound that she'd never associated with sex, but that made her entire body tighten with need.

Being with Stavros wouldn't be like any experience she'd had before. Not even close. Being with Stavros would be…

A really bad idea.

She froze, their lips still connected, her fingers curled into the fabric on his shirt. "Stop," she said.

He did. Immediately. He moved away from her, his expression as dazed as she felt. "That's not what I came up here for."

"What did you come up here for?" she asked, her words shaky, her entire body shaky.

"I...don't know." He sounded shocked. Dumbfounded. She wasn't sure if it was a comfort or an insult.

"But not for...that?"

He shook his head. "I'd ruled that out as a possibility."

"But you'd...thought about it?"

"Not a good question."

"You're right about that."

He took a step away from her. "It's understandable that we're attracted to each other."

"Totally," she said.

"But that doesn't mean we can act on it."

"No," she said, while her body screamed at her to change her answer.

And what would happen if she did? Professional suicide. And for what?

Sex for her had become all about failure. About shortcomings. All of hers on display when she was literally naked and as vulnerable as she could possibly be. She couldn't get pregnant. She couldn't even orgasm properly. As her husband had told her during one particularly ugly argument, there was literally no point in having sex with her. He'd said at the time his right hand was better company.

"I'm sorry."

"Oh, don't," she said, her lip curling in disgust, her body rebelling. "Don't apologize for kissing me, please, that's just... I'm not going to let you do that. Act like there was something...wrong with it." There was always something wrong.

"It was inappropriate."

Annoyance spiked inside her. "You're acting like you

compromised my maidenly virtue, or something. That's long gone so you don't need to worry."

"You are working for me right now."

"Not exactly."

"No matter what, it was wrong of me to do it. You're trying to help me find a wife, I'm paying you to do it. I have no right to charge in your room and kiss you."

"I kissed you back," she said, crossing her arms beneath her breasts, unwilling, unable to back down. Because she would not be treated like she was a victim in this. She was tired of being a victim. And she would not show him how much she was affected by it, either.

His expression was almost pained. "Don't remind me."

"That good?"

"If you keep talking I'll be tempted to kiss you again simply to quiet you down."

"You say the sweetest things, Prince Stavros. I am pudding at your feet." Oh, she could have cried. She was so relieved to have those sassy words fall out of her mouth. She needed them. Needed the distance and protection they would provide.

His jaw tensed, his lips, so soft and sensual a moment before, thinned. "You are...infuriating."

"And you like it," she said. "Wonder what that says about you?"

For a moment, he looked like he might grab her again. Might pull her up against his hard body and press his lips to hers.

Instead, he turned away from her.

"I'm going to call the girls. See when they can come out here. You're paying, naturally," she said. She didn't know why she'd chosen to tell him that. Only that the temptation to make him stay a bit longer had been stronger than it should have been.

He stopped and turned. "Naturally."

"See you tomorrow then."

"I'll be busy."

"So will I. I have other clients to do consultations with." She was still stalling. Still trying to keep him close.

He ignored her last statement and turned away again, heading down the hall. She let out a breath and walked back into her room, shutting the door behind her.

She picked up her iPad and opened up her file for Stavros.

Good kisser. Amazing body.

She deleted both as soon as she wrote them. If only she could delete it from her memory so easily.

CHAPTER SIX

THE women had arrived. Victoria, Amy and Cherry. Beautiful, polished and royal. They were wearing sleek, expensive-looking clothing, their hair perfectly coiffed, their makeup expertly applied.

They were perfectly beautiful. Perfectly boring.

Stavros surveyed the three women in their spot on the balcony. He felt like he was being featured on a bad reality television show. It was suddenly hard to breathe.

He'd been around some in his thirty-three years. Some people might call him a playboy, he preferred to think he was taking advantage of the physical while ignoring the emotional. Even so, facing three women who had marriage on their minds was out of his realm of experience.

Jessica was not out there with him, not there to run interference and give him a time limit for how long each woman could speak to him.

Victoria spoke first. "It's nice to meet you," she said. "I apologize if you weren't expecting me…us." He could tell she was irritated to be sharing the terrace with the other two women, who clearly felt the same way she did.

"Of course you were expected," he said, opting for diplomacy. Though he hoped, fervently, that they were staying at a hotel in Piraeus and not in the villa. Two was company, five would be a nightmare.

Especially considering that kiss he'd shared with Jessica and all the options it was making him contemplate. Again.

Victoria smiled, saccharine and a bit false, though, again given the situation, he hardly blamed her. His own smile was just as fake.

Cherry—at least he was assuming she was Cherry based on Jessica's description—spoke next. "I waited down at the airport for quite a while."

"I apologize," he said.

"I didn't have to wait," Victoria said, her expression a bit superior as she looked at the other two women.

"Because your plane landed last," Amy said, sniffing slightly.

He heard the click of high heels behind him and turned, a rush of heat filling him as Jessica came walking out onto the terrace.

"Sorry, ladies, I didn't realize you'd arrived." She smiled widely and he could sense the women in front of him relaxing as Jessica drew closer. She put her hands on her hips, pushing her full skirt in, revealing a bit of those luscious curves. "I had told the driver to bring you to your hotel. I apologize for the confusion."

Efharisto con theo.

He didn't want three women, all vying for position as queen, under the same roof. At least not one he was beneath. Not a very good thought to have, since it was very possible one of the three could be sharing his home, his bed, for the rest of their lives.

They could spend the rest of their lives smiling falsely at each other. He didn't know where the thought came from, and he didn't know why it filled him with an emotion that he could only identify as terror.

He appraised the three sleek women in front of him. All different in coloring, height and shape. He tried, he tried very hard, to find one that appealed to him more than the others.

A blonde, a brunette and a redhead...

He could not find anything especially appealing.

Until Jessica appeared on the balcony. That made fire in his blood, heat pooling in his gut, coursing down to his groin. His lips burned with the memory of her kiss. Just a kiss. Something that, for a man of his experience, should mean nothing. And yet, it had seemed the height of sensuality. The pinnacle of pleasure.

More than that, his heart had burned. And it hadn't hurt. It hadn't been unpleasant at all. He didn't know what that meant.

"Since you're here, I think we should have a drink before you're taken back into the city." Jessica was in control, her smile unshakable, her composure solid. "Does that suit?"

Amy looked like she might protest, about the drink or being taken back into the city, but instead, she nodded along with the others. Jessica turned and went back into the villa, undoubtedly to give the order for drinks to be served.

The three women stared at him, doe-eyed. An indistinct blur of beauty that meant nothing more to him than the scenery. Possibly less. "Excuse me for a moment," he said, turning and following Jessica. "Jessica…"

She whirled around, hands on her head. "I am so sorry."

"You are?"

"Yes. I don't really like all the three of the women to be together and…this…all right, this isn't really going according to my system. But it's okay. We'll improvise. We'll all have a drink, we'll chat, tomorrow you can choose one to go on a dinner date with. Does that work?"

"Fine," he said, amused by how quickly her composure had evaporated once they were out of sight of the other women.

"Really, this just makes it all seem a bit…"

"Like a reality television show?"

"Yes. And also a bit crass. And I'm sorry. But they all know the drill, so while it's awkward, they knew that they weren't the only people who had put in to be considered for this match."

He leaned against the wall. "So how exactly do women find you?"

"I advertise. In a discreet manner of course, but I've managed to put together a select group of men and women. When someone comes to me looking for a match, I let those who meet the qualifications know, and then they respond and let me know if they're interested. Simple."

"In a complex sort of way."

She raised both eyebrows, her expression haughty. "Well, it works anyway."

"So how many of these women you've shown me haven't made the final cut with other men?"

She sniffed. "Almost all of them. Where is the wine?"

"Which ones?"

"Only Victoria has never asked to be entered in for consideration yet. You were the first one she showed interest in."

"Setting her sights high?"

She kept her focus on her hunt for beverages. "Wine?"

"I mean that as far as status goes, not really saying I surpass the other men in terms of other qualities."

"Right. Where is the wine?"

He chuckled and reached behind her, pulling a bottle from the built in rack above her head. "Will a merlot do?" He took glasses from the rack as well, holding them by the stems.

"Fine." She reached up and took the bottle from his hand, then tilted it in his direction. "We should…" She gestured in the direction of the terrace. "Because I don't want them to scratch each other's eyes out or anything."

"Remind me again why you thought this would be a good idea?"

She frowned. "Well, it seemed logical. It sort of followed how I do things…it's just…it not being a big event sort of closes everything in a bit more."

"Yeah."

He took the bottle from her hand and led the way back out onto the terrace. Victoria, Cherry and Amy were standing at the far end of the terrace, a healthy bit of distance between each them so that they didn't have to engage in conversation with one another.

He set the glasses down on a small round bistro table and opened the bottle, pouring a substantial portion into each glass.

"Drinks," he said, lifting one for himself. They would need them.

The women advanced and each took their wine. The silence was awkward, oppressive. He hated this, he was starting to realize. It was the first thing he could remember hating in a long time. He hadn't had an emotion so strong in…years.

He hadn't thought he would mind this situation. Because he didn't want a wife, not in a particular sense. Marriage for him would be something he did for his country. A distant affair, and that was how it had to be. He knew—he'd seen—that love, emotional attachment, could overpower strong men. Bring them to their knees. And if those men were in control of the country, they could bring the country down with them.

That was why he had to do it this way. That was why he had to keep everyone at a distance. Why he had to find a wife who would matter to the country, not to him.

Still, even with that in mind, being in the middle of the matchmaking process was as enjoyable as being boiled alive. His flirtatious manner was harder to hold on to than he could ever remember it being before.

Ultimately, it was Jessica, her quick wit and sparkling laugh, that saved the night. She engaged everyone in conversation and managed to make things seem easy. Easier at least.

By the time his marriage candidates had been sent off in the limo, the knot in his gut had eased. Though, it could have been due to the wine and not just Jessica's lightning-quick wit.

As soon as the women were out of sight Jessica let out a loud breath and lifted her wineglass to her lips, tilting her head back and knocking the rest of the contents in. "That was vile. Worse than vile."

"You're good at covering up how you feel."

"So are you," she said. "Image. It's important to both of us, right?"

"I have to put on a good front for my people." Except he hadn't thought of it as a front before. He'd simply thought of himself as empty of anything but confidence. Empty of anything unimportant. If something needed to be done, he saw it done.

"And I have to put on a calm front for my clients."

"Then why is it you're letting me in on just how stressed out that made you?"

She grimaced. "Well, for all intents and purposes, we're roommates at the moment and I have to let my hair down at some point in the day, so to speak. For another, you've licked my lips and that puts you slightly over the line of 'usual client.' Slightly."

"You don't let all your clients lick your lips?" he asked. A strange tightness invaded his chest, his stomach. Jealousy.

Possessiveness. The image of all of her clients getting the
sort of special treatment he had been on the receiving end
of made him want to pull her to him again, to make sure
she didn't forget what it was like to be kissed by him. To
make sure she never forgot.

That was as foreign as all the other emotions she'd
brought out in him over the past few days. Jealousy im-
plied some sort of special connection, and a fear of that
connection being threatened.

He gritted his teeth, fought against the tightness in his
chest. Flirting. That would put the distance back between
them. Something light. Sexual.

"Hardly," she said. Unable to read his mood, she kept
her tone casual. "Indulge me, though, since I've now confessed that I don't kiss my other clients. What exactly are
you hiding?" She tilted her head, her green eyes assessing.
Far too assessing for his taste. Too sincere.

It made it impossible to find that false front. Made him
feel something shift deep inside himself.

"No skeletons in my closet," he said. "But of course I
have to live a certain way, conduct myself in a certain way."

"You aren't exactly a traditional ruler."

"It's not just tradition. It's about instilling confidence.
Showing stability. Emotion…that has no place. I must be
charming, confident, at ease at all times."

"I've never heard a whispered rumor that you were anything but."

He looked out into the darkness, at the black ocean,
moonlight glittering across the choppy surface. "I know.
Because I don't slip up. Ever."

He had, though. He had slipped up with her. He had let
go of his control, control he'd been forced to cultivate when
he'd been named heir to the throne. He'd let go of it completely in those moments his lips had touched hers. Not

control against physical desire, but the control he kept so tightly over his feelings.

Jessica laughed, a sad, hollow sound. "I'm certain I do. Sometimes."

"What about you, Ms. Carter?" he said. "What are you hiding?" He turned to her, studying her face in the dim light. It seemed imperative to know her secrets. And he wasn't certain why it would be. But just like last night, he was going to let his guard drop. Just for a moment. Just to follow that heavy, aching feeling in his chest. To give it some satisfaction.

The corners of her mouth twitched slightly. "If I told you, I'd have to kill you."

Warmth spread through him. In him. An alien feeling. One he was compelled to chase for the moment. "And that would create an international incident."

"It would prick my conscience as well, so maybe I should keep it to myself," she said, a small curve in her lips. It wasn't really a smile, though. It was too sad for that. "Better question, if you could be anything, I mean, if the whole world was open to you, what would you be?"

He frowned. "If I wasn't in line to rule Kyonos?"

"If you weren't royal at all. If you could have anything you desired, without obligation, what would you do?"

It was the thing he never let himself wonder. The alternate reality that wasn't even allowed in his dreams. But he was cheating now. Cheating on his own standards for himself.

For a fleeting moment, he had a vision of a life that was his own. A life with a woman of his choosing, in a home of his choosing. With children who wouldn't know the pain, the responsibility of a royal lineage depending on them. With love.

He shoved the image aside. "I would run my corporation," he said. He had a sudden image of sailing a ship around the world and wondered if he'd told the truth.

"Would you get married?" she asked, a strange tone to her voice.

"Yes," he said, the answer almost surprising him. But in that little, warm hint of fantasy, there had been a wife. There had been kids. And it wasn't hard to breathe. "Yes," he said again.

"Hmm." She turned and walked to the end of the terrace, resting her hands on the railing.

He followed her, standing behind her, watching the sea breeze tug wisps of hair from her updo, letting them fall around her neck. He wanted to brush them aside. To kiss her shoulder. Her neck. Not just because he wanted her, but to feel connected to her.

A deadly desire.

"Why do you do it?" she asked. "Why is this so important?"

She was asking for more honesty. For answers he wasn't sure he had. "I... When my mother died things fell apart. And the one thing that seemed real, that seemed to matter, was Kyonos. It was the one thing I could fix. The one place I could...matter."

As he spoke the words, he realized that they were true. That every change he'd made, every effort he'd put forth, had been not just about helping his country, but about finding new purpose for himself.

"What about you?" he asked, ready to shift the spotlight off of himself.

She didn't speak for a long time. When she did, she spoke slowly, cautiously. "In this scenario, reality isn't playing a part, right?"

"Right," he said, voice rough. He waited for her next words, anticipated them like a man submerged beneath the waves anticipated breaking the surface, desperate to take a breath.

She lowered her head, her eyes on her hands. "I would be a wife. A mother..." Her voice broke on the last word. "And maybe I would still do this, or maybe not. I don't know if I would...need it. But...I would be a mother."

She pushed off from the railing. "Back to reality," she said, trying to smile. Failing. "I'm going to bed."

He nodded, watching as she walked past him.

I would be a mother.

There was something so sad, so defeated in the admission. It made his chest tighten, and he couldn't pinpoint why. He'd never had someone else's feelings inhabit his body in this way. But he was certain that's what was happening. That the oppressive weight that had just invaded him was the same sadness that filled her.

Maybe Jessica wasn't as happily divorced as she appeared to be. And maybe she wasn't quite as hard as she appeared to be, either.

She was running interference for Stavros and his harem today, and she wasn't all that thrilled about it. It was getting harder to chuck other women in his direction when she just wanted to throw herself at him.

Not happening, but still. She was so envious of her clients that she was developing a twitch.

And for heaven's sake, she never should have said all that about being a mother. Should never have asked him what he wanted. Should never have tried to get to know him. Because it didn't matter. It just didn't. There was no point in suspending reality, even for a moment.

There was no escaping reality. You couldn't outrun it. You could try but eventually it would bite you in the ass. She knew that. She knew it really, really well. She'd tried to ignore how often she and her husband went to their separate corners of the house. She'd tried to ignore his touch at night, and when she couldn't, she tried to ignore his total disregard for her pain. She'd even tried to ignore his outright berating of her. The screaming and anger and hateful words.

No, there was no point in ignoring that kind of thing. The facts were simple. Stavros needed certain things, she didn't have any of them.

Why was she even thinking about that crap? She didn't have time for it. She had a gaggle of women to manage for the whole day.

She blew out a breath and slipped her oversize sunglasses onto her face, tightening her hold on her latte. She had gotten them all booked into a luxury salon in Piraeus, and they were all safely getting massaged and waxed as she stood out on the crowded, narrow streets drinking her coffee.

Stavros was coming soon. He was meeting the group of them for a quick lunch and tour around the city, and then he would be selecting the woman who would accompany him on a private date for the evening.

And it would be up to Jessica to send the other two off without making them feel like it really was some low-rent reality television show.

Jessica wasn't used to feeling like things were out of her control. Not since that moment four years ago when she'd taken back the reins of her life. She liked to feel like she had everything managed. Like her little universe was in the palm of her hand.

It was an illusion, and she knew it, but she still liked it.

Since Stavros, she didn't even have her illusion.

What was it about him that reminded her...that reminded her she was a woman? Not just on the surface, but really and truly. With a woman's desires, no matter how hard life had tried to wring them out of her.

Oh, dear…right on time. The master of her rekindled sexual needs was striding toward her. Cream-colored jacket and trousers, shirt open at the collar. She did love a man who knew how to dress. A Mediterranean sex god with very expensive taste.

He also had two dark-suited members of security flanking him and discreetly parting the crowd so that His Majesty wouldn't be jostled.

Not that Stavros ever behaved that way. He didn't act like a spoiled prince who would be able to feel a pea through fifty mattresses, not even close. He acted like a man who carried the weight of a nation on his shoulders.

More than that, he acted like a man who intended to support the weight of that nation for the rest of his life. A man prepared to tailor his every decision to suit that responsibility.

"Hello, Jessica," he said, a smile curving his lips.

"Prince Stavros," she said, reverting because last night had gotten a bit too intimate and she had no desire to go there again. Well, that was a lie. She did want to go there again. But she couldn't.

"Demoted, I see."

"What?"

"Back to a title."

"Oh…" Why did he have to notice all these little things about her? Why did he have to care at all? "Sorry."

"How are things going?"

"Good. Great. Looking forward to you thinning the herd tonight."

"You make it sound like there are a lot more than three."

She sighed. "They feel like more than three. In my experience, the women haven't been so catty. But then, I normally don't do this with them in such close proximity to each other. I've also never tried to match a crown prince."

He looked past her, into the spa. "Let's leave them in there."

"What?" She looked behind her.

"If we hurry, they won't know I was here."

She laughed. "You're not serious."

He frowned. "No. I'm not. Things are getting... I need to make a decision."

"Because of Eva?" she asked, remembering his mood at his sister's wedding.

"Everyone in Kyonos was happy for Eva. They love to see their princess in love. But I have to be sure that I make them feel like there's stability."

"You've been the rock for Kyonos for a long time," she said, not quite sure why she felt compelled to offer him... not comfort...support, maybe.

"And I will continue to do it. With a wife by my side."

"A most suitable wife."

"Yes." He looked back in the spa. "Will they be done soon?"

"Soon.

"It's not too late to go another route," she said, not sure why she was offering her client an out from a program she publicly professed, and privately believed, to be the best way to find a mate.

He shrugged. "Why would I?"

"You could still fall in love." She wrapped both hands around her paper cup and hugged it close to her body.

"No. I can't."

"I'm sure you could. What if you met the perfect woman and she was wholly suitable?"

He shook his head. "It isn't that I don't think it's possible. It's that I won't. Love weakens a leader. You know of Achilles and his heel, I assume?"

"Of course."

He frowned, his expression intense. "One weakness is all it takes to crumble a man who is strong in all other areas. And a weak leader can destroy what was a strong nation. I will never have part in that."

He was serious again. Like last night. Not a hint of flirtation. She was starting to wonder if that was really him at all. Or if it was who he thought he was supposed to be.

"Is that really what you think?"

"I know it. I saw it happen, in my family, in Kyonos. When my mother died everything fell apart. My father could not function. He… We made Xander the scapegoat for it, all because grief could only give way to anger. I had to set it aside. I had to move on for the good of the country. It took my father years to do it. He is a king, he did not have the luxury of grief, or pain. It's different for us."

She studied his face, so hard and impassive, as though it were carved from marble. "Feeling pain is the only way I know to deal with it." Sometimes she wondered if she clung to pain. If she turned it over and dissected more than she needed to. If she used it to protect herself.

"I have gotten to the point where I don't feel it at all. Kyonos comes first, and everything else comes second. That will include a wife. She'll have to understand that. She'll have to understand that her role is not to love me, but to love my country."

Bone deep sadness assaulted her. He deserved more than that. More than this.

Her phone buzzed and she pulled up her text messages.

We're done. Where are you?

The message was from Victoria.
Out front. She typed out the note and then hit Send.
"They're done," she said. "Brace yourself."

He straightened his shoulders, his expression changing, that wicked charm back in place. She had to work hard to suppress a smile.

As if on cue the three women walked out of the spa, sunglasses fixed firmly on flawless faces. Victoria was the first to spot Stavros, the first to smile widely. "Prince Stavros. How lovely."

Like she was surprised. Like she hadn't been briefed by Jessica early that morning.

"Lovely to see you, Victoria," he said, inclining his head. "Cherry, Amy."

Cherry and Amy didn't look thrilled at being afterthoughts, but they managed to smile, too, and offer platitudes about what a lovely day it was.

"I've made reservations at a café down by the water," he said.

"Sounds lovely," Amy said, taking her chance to be the first to speak.

"My car is just this way," he said, leading down the narrow street and to a black limo idling at the curb. The security detail opened the back doors on both sides. The women slid in and took their positions on the bench seats that ran the length of the car.

Jessica got in and sat on the bench facing them, and Stavros slid in beside her. The doors closed and the air-conditioning provided immediate relief from the heat. Or, rather, it would have, if Stavros himself wasn't so hot.

A thick, awkward silence settled into the air and Jessica worked to find her social ease. She was good with people. It was one of her strengths. But Stavros had her in the throes of her first sexual attraction in years and his potential brides were sitting a foot away.

It was more awkward than any situation had the right to be.

"I..." She cleared her throat. "I'm really looking forward to lunch."

"I'm looking forward to dinner," said Cherry, flashing Stavros a smile.

From awkwardness to greater awkwardness.

"I imagine everyone will be eating dinner tonight," Jessica said, a bit too brightly. *Some will be eating alone, though.*

Stavros laughed...easy, charming. False. He did that so well. No matter the situation he seemed to be in control. More than that, he seemed to distance himself. The flirtier and friendlier he seemed, the less present he actually was. And that seemed to be his default setting.

Not always. Her mind flashed back to the kiss. That hadn't been emotionless at all. Or distant. That had been... amazing. And wild. She sneaked a peek at him from the corner of her eyes, her line of sight connecting her with the strong column of his throat. She was willing to bet he tasted like salt. Clean skin and man.

"I'm certain everyone will," he said, earning a delicate blush from Cherry.

The limo stopped and Jessica nearly said a prayer of thanks out loud. "We're here!"

The doors opened and they filed out. The restaurant was at the harbor, the seating area extending over the pier. Boats, ranging in size from dinghies to yachts, filled the horizon. Seagulls screeched nearby, landing near tables, fighting over crumbs, showing no respect for their otherwise elegant surroundings.

Jessica made sure everyone ordered wine with their

lunch. Heaven knew they would need it to get through the afternoon.

They made appropriate small talk while they waited for their orders to be filled and Jessica cringed inside as she watched the patented disinterest in Stavros's eyes grow more and more pronounced.

She wanted to pinch him. She couldn't fix him up if he didn't even try to like the women she introduced him to.

She caught his gaze and treated him to a hard stare. A glimmer of amusement appeared in the depths of his dark eyes. She didn't even want to know what he was thinking.

When everyone had their food, Stavros leaned in, his very best charming-politician smile on his face. How had she not noticed before? How fake it was. How much it wasn't him at all. "I know this is a bit unusual. But I think it's best to think of it as a job interview. I hope no one finds that offensive. We have all signed up to have Jessica's help finding a suitable spouse, have we not?"

Jessica wanted to hit him. Except none of the women seemed offended at all. They should have been. His mercenary assessment should have made them all angry. They should have poured wine in his lap.

They didn't, they simply nodded.

"The reality is, my country needs very specific things from a queen. That's my top priority."

"Naturally," Victoria said. "We're all far too practical to think this is going to be a love match."

Cherry nodded, and Amy only stared into her glass.

"Then the rejection should not be personal, either," he said, his charm never slipping. He was firm, yet still perfectly engaging. She didn't understand how he did it. She didn't understand what he was doing, and yet, he was doing it.

"This is really lovely," Jessica said, looking around them. "Isn't it lovely?"

Amy nodded. "It really is."

She chattered on about the scenery and the food, anything to dispel the lingering scent of that horrible honesty of Stavros's. They managed to make it through the meal and get the women deposited at their hotel without it appearing again.

That left just the two of them alone in the limo for the ride back to the villa.

"And what was that?" she asked.

"What was what?" He was positioned across from her, and he still felt too close, because now there was no one in the back with them to help diffuse the tension.

"That. The whole thing about it being a job interview. Didn't I tell you to keep your candor to yourself? Or just tell me if you have something so honest to say."

"They didn't seem to mind. Anyway, I had to make a choice about tonight, about which one of the three to continue seeing. If that, the clinical nature of this, is going to bother them, they should leave now. I'm not doing this for romance."

"I know…"

"And now so do they. If any one of them wants to leave they better do it now, I don't have time to mess around with the future of my country. I told you already, I need a queen who understands that her loyalty will be to Kyonos."

"Still…geez. Don't underestimate the power of a little sweet talk."

"I of all people know about sweet talk, as you should know. I do have a reputation. But I'm not going to deceive anyone that's involved in this."

"I appreciate that. I wasn't talking deceit. Just…sugar-coating."

"I didn't think you did sugarcoating," he said, his dark eyes locked with hers.

"Um…well, I don't…I mean not with you, but you have to know how to talk to women."

"You think you know how to talk to women better than I do? How many women have you dated?"

She crossed her arms beneath her breasts. "Zero, but I *am* a woman so I win."

"This isn't about tricking someone into marrying me because they want to be a princess and live in a castle and have their happily-ever-after. They can want a title, but they have to be worthy of it. They have to know what it means. They have to realize I'm a busy man and that love isn't high on my list of priorities. It's not even on the list of options. For that reason, I thought it was important I spelled it out."

She looked out the window, her throat tightening. For one moment, just for a moment, she pictured Stavros without the obligations. What would it be like for him? If he could have been free to do what he wanted? If he could have had that wife and the children that he'd seen in his mind's eye last night while they were talking? Would his expectations be different?

Would he have loved that wife? If he didn't feel like a nation was dependent on his emotional strength, would he have given himself over to love? Would he have focused his fearsome loyalty on his family?

The thought of it, of what it would be like to be the woman on the receiving end of all that intensity, filled her with a kind of bone-deep longing.

Get a grip, Jess. Even if he was free, she wouldn't be the woman for him. He had goals, dreams and desires that weren't about his wife, or who she was, but what she could offer. And they were things she couldn't offer. She knew all about trying to be perfect for someone when she fell so far short of it. She could never do it again.

"I respect that," she said.

"Victoria."

"What?"

"It's Victoria. She's the one I want to see again." His voice didn't hold any particular enthusiasm.

She felt like she'd been sucker punched. And she wasn't sure why. "Did you...have a lightning-attraction thing?"

A muscle in his cheek jumped. "She's lovely. More than that, I think she's a bit...well, she seemed unemotional." He didn't sound too enthusiastic and she hated the small, ridiculous part of herself that liked that. The part that wanted Stavros to be dwelling on their kiss, and not on his attraction to another woman.

Even if that other woman was the one he might potentially marry.

"Victoria is... She's very smart. And I'm certain she would do a lot of good as queen." Victoria wasn't just smart, she was brilliant. And, Stavros was right, a bit on the unemotional end of things. She was looking for an opportunity to better herself, and to make an impact on the world.

Jessica had been trying to talk Victoria into considering a few of her previous clients, but Victoria hadn't been interested. Because she'd clearly been holding out for better. And had found it in Stavros.

Well, nice for some.

For you, too, she tried to remind herself, but herself wasn't listening. Herself was sulking a little bit.

"Great, I'll call down to the hotel later."

"I'll do it," he said. "If you give me her room number."

"Can't," she said, the word escaping before she could think better of it.

"Why?"

Her stomach tightened to a painful degree. "No sex, remember?"

"I'm not going to have sex with her, not at this point. I'm going to call and ask her to dinner."

She cleared her throat, ignoring the little surge her heart had taken when he'd said the word *sex*. Because when he said it was so…evocative. Husky male tones wrapped in an exotic accent. It made her think of tangled limbs and heavy breathing and…

And what? Like she was some great sensual goddess? Like she would be able to enjoy being with him? Like he would enjoy being with her? Her throat ached and she couldn't fathom the sudden onslaught of emotion. What was wrong with her?

"Yeah, I'll call Amy and Cherry then and just let them know that…I'll let them know they can return home."

"At their leisure. They can stay in the city for a few more days if they wish. I'll continue to pay their expenses for as long they remain here. An extended holiday doesn't seem too unreasonable."

"Ah, so you'll ask Victoria out but I have to break it off with the other two?"

"As I said earlier, it's just a job interview. And only one candidate can get hired, so to speak."

"Right." She leaned back in the chair and flexed her fingers, curling them into fists and letting her manicured nails dig into her palms.

There was no reason at all the thought of Stavros going on a date with Victoria should make her feel like she might be sick.

But it did. She couldn't deny that it did.

She was seriously losing it.

"Well, if I don't see you again before your date...break a leg."

He smiled, but his eyes held a strange, unreadable expression. "I'll see you. After at least."

No. "See you then."

CHAPTER SEVEN

THERE was nothing wrong with Victoria. She was beautiful, she was pleasant. Smart. She would make a wonderful queen. Over dinner she'd talked at great length concerning how passionate she was about charities, starting foundations and visiting hospitals.

She possessed all the qualities he required for a bride.

Yet as he thought of binding himself to her, he felt nothing. No matter how hard he tried. He felt like he was being suffocated. As if the weight of the crown would physically crush him.

Don't think of marriage. Think of sex.

If he could find a connection with her on that level, then maybe nothing else would matter. If he could flirt and put them both at ease, put a wall between them, maybe the tightness in his throat would abate.

When the limo stopped in front of the hotel she looked at him from beneath her lashes, her open, friendly expression changing. Seduction, he decided, was her intent. Good. He knew the game. Often, he relished the game.

So, why didn't he feel anything? Nothing. Not even the slightest twinge of interest in his stomach. When she cocked her head to the side and licked her lips, there was no answering tug in his groin. Indeed, there was no signal coming from south of his belt at all. It was as though that member of his body hadn't registered her existence.

He was a man, a man with a healthy appetite for sex. And she was, on paper, a sexually attractive woman. What he should be doing was pressing her back against the soft leather seat and claiming her soft pink lips.

His body rejected the idea while his mind replaced the image of a rosy pink mouth with one painted in temptation red. And with that image came a tightness in his chest, his heart pounding harder, his mind suddenly filled with Jessica.

"I had a nice time at dinner," he said.

"So did I," she said, cocking her head to the side even farther. Why was it that some women thought affecting the mannerisms of a cocker spaniel was sexy?

Except, usually, he would find this sexy. He just didn't now. No use pretending he didn't know why.

"Good night," he said, opening the door to the limo and stepping out into the cool night. He held the door for her, giving as strong of a hint as he could.

She frowned and slid out, her body on the opposite side of the door to his. "I had a…a really nice time." Her blue eyes were locked with his, her intentions obvious.

"So you said."

"I appreciate you taking me out."

"We'll go out again. When I'm through with my business here." Where was the flirtation? Why couldn't he even pretend that he was interested? Whatever he felt for Jessica, it shouldn't have the power to reach him here and now. It shouldn't be able to control his thoughts and actions. That was the sort of thing he'd spent most of his adult life fighting.

"Oh...okay." She smiled. "That's good, right?"

It should have been. But he didn't have any sort of positive feeling about it. "You're a...nice woman, Victoria."

Nice? Where the hell had his seduction skills gone?

"Thank you. You're a nice man, Stavros." She cleared her throat. "Good night, then?"

"Good night," he said.

She stepped out of the way of the door and he closed it firmly. He would walk her into the hotel, as was the appropriate thing to do, but that was all.

She looked at him one more time in the lobby of the hotel, requesting a kiss, and when he took a step back he could have sworn he saw a fleeting hint of relief in her eyes.

"Hopefully we'll see each other again soon," she said.

"Hopefully," he said, turning and leaving her in the lobby.

He felt no such hope. He would see her again though. Just because something in him was off at the moment didn't mean she wasn't the right candidate for the job. For the marriage.

He grimaced, lifted his hand to loosen his tie, which suddenly felt like a hangman's noose.

Victoria was a sound choice.

He gritted his teeth. Yes, she was a sound choice. It didn't matter that he desired someone else. Desire, no matter how strong, did not have a say in the future of his country. Desire could not shake his resolve.

He closed his eyes for a moment, clenched his hands into fists to disguise the unsteadiness in his fingers. It was only lust. Nothing special. Nothing important. A picture of Jessica flashed through his mind and there was an answering kick in his gut.

In spite of his intentions, desire seemed to be shaking

him from the inside out. And what he really didn't want to believe was that a whole lot more than desire was making him tremble.

Jessica wrapped her arms around herself and turned away from the view of the ocean, leaning against the rail of the terrace, the salted breeze blowing at her back, tangling in her hair. She wondered what Stavros was doing. If his date with Victoria has been successful.

Part of her hoped that it had been. He could marry her and they could have gorgeous, royal babies that could inherit the throne of Kyonos. They could be all sexy and royal together and she could go back to her empty house and contemplate the merit of getting a cat.

Yes, that was a good plan. A solid plan. She could name her cat Mittens.

"And how was your evening?"

She turned and her breath caught in her throat, forcing a sharp, gasping sound. Stavros was in the doorway, his black tie draped over his shoulder, the first three buttons of his shirt undone, the sleeves pushed up to his elbows.

He looked like he'd been undressed. She tried to smile while her stomach sank slowly into her toes, jealousy an acrid thing that ate at her insides, working its way out.

"I think that's my line," she said. Her words scraped over her dry throat.

"Lovely. Not nearly as lovely as you are. But lovely." A smile curved his lips and he stepped fully onto the deck, closing some of the distance between them.

There was something strange about his manner. Something too slack. Too easy. "Have you been drinking?"

"Not even a little. But you do make me feel a bit light-headed."

"Seriously. What the heck, Stavros?"

"Careful, *agápe,* you'll make me think I've lost my touch."

"What did I tell you about not flirting with me?" Rather than the sort of shaky, sexy unease she usually felt when he flirted with her, she only felt anger. He had no right to do this to her. No right at all. He had been on a date with another woman. A date that, ideally, would be the beginning of a 'til-death sort of relationship.

"You told me not to." He stepped closer to her, his movements lithe. Graceful. Like a panther. "But I find I can't help myself."

"Then get some help from an outside source," she growled, tightening her arms around herself.

"You are upset with me?" he asked, a boyish, teasing glint in his eye.

"Yes, I am upset with you. I don't understand you. You kiss me, you act mad about it, you apologize, you go on a date with another woman and now you're flirting."

"Victoria was fine."

"Fine?"

"Adequate. I should like to see her again."

"What? That's all?"

"I would like to marry her," he said between clenched teeth.

"And you came out here flirting with me?"

He shrugged. "I told you why I'm doing this. It has nothing to do with personal feelings or excitement on my part and everything to do with getting things in order for Kyonos."

"Great," she said, annoyance deserting her, replaced by a sadness she had no business feeling.

"I prefer it when you smile," he said, injecting a playful note to his voice.

"I don't feel like smiling." She turned away from him, her focus pinned decidedly onto the scenery.

"Why do you do this?"

"Why do I do what?" she asked, not looking at him as she responded.

"Why do you make it impossible for me to reach you?"

"Why are you trying?"

"Because I can't take a breath without thinking of you," he said, his voice suddenly real. Raw.

"I don't..."

"Jessica," he said, regaining some of his composure, "you know my situation. My obligations. But that doesn't mean we can't see where our attraction takes us."

"Yes, Stavros, yes, it does mean that," she said, panic fluttering in her chest. Panic and a desperate desire to believe the words he'd just spoken.

His dark brows locked together. "That kiss...it haunts me. It's eating at me. I need..." He sucked in a sharp breath. "I need you. Tell me you need me, too."

"I..." She shook her head. "It doesn't matter if I do."

His expression shifted, a veil dropping, revealing unguarded hunger. Stark and nearly painful to witness. "Let's pretend that it does." The desperation in his tone, the raw need, was beyond her. And yet it called to her, echoed inside of her. "Let's pretend, like we did the other night, that none of the other stuff exists. That I am just a man. And you are just a woman. A woman I desire above all else."

She sucked in a breath that tore at her lungs, leaving her raw and bleeding inside, and tried to keep the tears from falling. How could he tempt her like this? "Stavros...that's the problem, all of that, that stuff we tried to ignore? It is real. And we can't pretend it's not. It won't change anything."

"Tonight it doesn't have to be real," he said, his voice dark, tortured.

"I am not your best bet for a last-minute, commitment-phobic fling," she admonished. "I am the last woman you should want for that."

"Why? The attraction between us is real. And you said yourself, it isn't as though you're a virgin. You're an experienced woman who knows what she wants."

There was no ease now. No flirtation. And he was harder to resist now because of it. Because this was real. What she'd witnessed when he'd first come out onto the terrace, that had been the fake. This was her evidence that he really did want her.

It was unfair. It was too much.

Anger, unreasonable and not entirely directed at Stavros, spilled over. "I'm pointless, don't you know? Can't you tell? I can't have a baby. I am a testosterone killer. I make a man feel like he isn't really a man. I can't be pleased sexually. Don't I know what that does to a man?" She knew she sounded crazy, hysterical. She didn't care. "I am cold. And frigid. A bitch who cares more for her own comfort than the dreams of her husband, than the hope of a family. Does that sound like the sort of woman you should have a fling with?"

She stood, her hands clenched at her sides, her breathing harsh. Speaking those words, giving voice to every terrible thing she'd been called, every horrible feeling that lived in her, made her feel powerful. It made her feel a little sick, too.

"Jessica...who said those things to you?" he asked, his voice rough.

"Who do you think?"

"Your husband?"

"Ex," she said, the word never tasting so sweet.

"He was wrong," he said.

"You don't know that. I just turned you down, didn't I?"

"And my ego remains intact."

"Just go."

"No. Help me understand," he said. It was a quiet statement, a simple gesture. It was more than anyone else had ever asked from her or offered her.

"This is one of those things men don't like to hear about. And by that I mean it contains the word *uterus* and pertains to that particular 'time of the month' that means a man can't get any action."

"Try me," he said, his dark eyes never leaving hers, his jaw tense. "Scare me, Jess. I dare you."

She forced a laugh. "Fine. I'll give it a shot. I had endometriosis. I might have it again someday, since it's still possible to have a flare-up. I don't know if you really know what that is but it's incredibly painful. I was one of the lucky ones for whom it was especially bad. It causes bleeding and…pain. Lots of pain. Lots of blood. For me it caused pain during sex. After orgasm. It could last for days for me. And…I started just not wanting to have desire anymore. I didn't even want to want sex. The reward was too fleeting for what I had to go through and…I rejected my husband. Often. I made him feel undesired. And you know what? He was."

She was sure that had to have done the trick. That had to have scared him. "I think that's your cue to turn and run."

He crossed his arms over his chest, his eyes never leaving hers. "I'm not a runner. Did it hurt you all the time?"

"Most of the time. I've had…" She always tripped over the word *hysterectomy* because there was something so defeating about it. "I had a procedure done to help, and it has, but…I haven't tested how well it worked in terms of… it still scares me."

"Jess..."

She was the one to take a step back. She shook her head. "It's not worth it, Stavros. For one night? It's not worth it. I'm way too much trouble. If you want one more fling before you get married make it with someone who's easy. And I don't mean that in the general sense. Make it with someone who actually wants sex."

The idea of trying it again, of failing again, destroyed her. It was more than just what it might mean to him. It was that she wanted it so much, and the thought of desiring yet one more thing that remained out of her reach was too painful to even consider.

She'd made success. She'd left her failures behind. There was no point repeating the same mistakes.

"I'm tired." She turned away from him and headed back to the house.

Stavros watched Jessica walk back into the villa, her arms wrapped around her body as though she were holding herself together with her own strength.

He felt numb. Numb and in pain all at once. He'd come out with the express purpose of seducing her. Of finding a way to put her in a category he was comfortable with. To embrace his sexual need and ignore the strange ache in his chest that seemed to appear whenever she was around.

It hadn't worked. She hadn't allowed the distance, and he certainly hadn't been able to retreat behind the security of flirtation, not after that admission.

What an ass he was for making her confess something like that.

She was right, he should run. He should take her advice and focus on his upcoming marriage. Or find a woman to help him burn through his pent-up sexual desire.

He took a heavy breath and walked into the house, heading for his office. He closed the door behind him and sat at his computer desk. He ought to email his father, at the very least, to let him know he was almost certain he was close to finding the future queen of Kyonos.

Instead he opened his internet browser and stared at the blinking cursor in the text box of the search engine.

Then he typed in *endometriosis.*

She wanted to cry, and she couldn't. She'd spent so long forcing herself to keep it together that now she actually wanted to take a moment to fall apart, she couldn't.

It was impossible to force tears.

She just lay on her bed and stared out the window at the moon glimmering on the surface of the ocean. It was the perfection of nature, beautiful and unspoiled. She would never understand why some things were fashioned so perfectly when she wasn't.

Why her body seemed to have been put together wrong when so many other people were made just right. Why she hadn't been able to just buck up and deal with it. Why the shame and failure still ate at her like a parasite.

And she wanted Stavros so much she could hardly stand living in her skin. She wanted to touch him, wanted to taste him. She wanted to kiss him again, to have all that passion directed at her. Mostly she wished she could go back and not tell him about her endometriosis. It had been so nice to have a man look at her like she was beautiful. To have him not see her as different from other women, not in a bad way, but in a way that made her seem special rather than damaged.

When he said she was different, he hadn't meant broken. He hadn't meant pointless. Worthless as a woman or a partner.

His perception of her had been a lie, sure. But it was one she would have been happy to live in for just a little while.

She closed her eyes and let their kiss play through her mind again. Allowed herself to relive what it had been like to feel the pressure of his hard body against hers. To feel his lips against hers, so hot and demanding. So unlike any man she'd ever kissed.

Desire coiled in her stomach, her heart beating faster, her body begging her for some sort of release. Release she'd denied herself for so long. Too long, maybe.

She sat up and balled her hands into fists, pushing against her closed eyes. Without thinking, she stood, her heart hammering as she slipped out into the hall and looked in the direction of Stavros's room. He would be in there by now, asleep.

And he wanted her. He'd said he did. It was such a rush. Such a shot of adrenaline. Pure, feminine pleasure. To be wanted. To want someone.

Her hands trembled and she shook them out, trying to steady them. Trying to steady herself. Easier said than done. She breathed in, then out again.

What if she could have a little bit of it? Something guaranteed. Something she couldn't fail at. She tried to swallow but the motion stuck in her dry throat. The idea of sleeping with Stavros was the most elating and terrifying thing she could imagine. To be so vulnerable to a man who was so perfect. To take a chance at failing again. At being revealed as not good enough.

Blood roared in her ears as she made her way to his room. She stopped and wiped her hands, damp with sweat, on her skirt. She knocked lightly on the door, not pausing to think because, if she did, she would have just turned and scurried back to the safety of her bed.

"Yes?" She heard Stavros's sleep-roughened voice from the other side of the door and she pushed it open.

He was propped up on his elbows, the sheets riding low

around his waist, revealing his chest. The moon glanced off the hard ridges of muscle, the valleys cast into shadow, giving his body the impression of cut stone.

He was utter perfection. Just as she thought, that was not the sort of chest she'd ever touched before. And she was dying to touch him. Aching for it. His beauty drew her in, but it also intimidated.

"I couldn't sleep," she said. So lame. "Obviously *you* could so maybe I shouldn't have come."

"I wasn't sleeping well," he said.

"That's good, I…" She took a step forward. "Can I?"

"Please," he said, his face half-hidden in shadow, his voice strained.

She sat on the edge of the bed and held her hand out in front of her, curling it into a fist, then flexing her fingers as she fought against indecision. Then she placed her palm on his chest and her breath caught as a shock of fire streaked through her veins.

He was so hot, his hair rough on her skin, his muscles hard, his skin smooth. She let her fingers drift down over his sculpted muscles, lightly skimming, following the ripple of his body.

She leaned in and kissed his lips. He remained frozen beneath her, his stomach rock-hard beneath her hand, his body wound tight. She could feel his tension, flowing from every tendon and into her fingertips. Hers to command. Hers to enjoy.

Maybe she couldn't have everything she wanted. But she could have some of it. He wanted her. And she could satisfy him. Without having to give up any power. Without being vulnerable. Without failing.

"What are you doing?" he asked, his forehead resting against hers, his lips a whisper away.

"If you have to ask, I must not be doing it right. It has

been a while, maybe protocol has changed?" She kissed his neck, tasted salt and sweat on his skin.

She let her hands slide down beneath the sheet, where she found him hard for her, a whole lot bigger than she'd anticipated. An involuntary rush of air hissed through her teeth, matching time with Stavros's sharp intake of breath as she curled her fingers around his erection.

In this, she was certain. Giving a man pleasure without taking any for herself had been a necessity in the latter days of her marriage. A desperate attempt to hold things together. A way to keep intimacy without having to deal with any physical discomfort.

She could do the same now, with Stavros. A way to have him without risking anything. It seemed so easy.

Except she was getting a lot hotter than she'd anticipated, and it made the thought of leaving his bed unsatisfied a lot less…satisfying than it had seemed a few moments earlier. Still, even without an orgasm she was enjoying this. Enjoying wanting him. Enjoying exploring his body.

It was a slice of what she wanted, and she'd learned to accept that that was how life was for her. Little tastes here and there of true pleasure, while the full experience stayed out of her reach. It would be enough, because it had to be.

She pressed a kiss to his pectoral muscle and down to his nipple, sliding her tongue over it, feeling it tighten beneath her touch.

His hand came up to the back of her head, fingers sifting through her hair. She smiled against his skin and continued to pepper kisses over his body. "You have the most incredible chest," she said, "among other things." She squeezed his shaft lightly. "I have never, ever, seen a man like you. Much less been close enough to have a taste. And I was really looking forward to it. You do not disappoint." She lifted her head and tugged the sheet down, exposing him. "Oh, no, you don't disappoint at all."

Her heart beat hard, echoing in her temples, at the apex of her thighs. He was amazing. Everything she'd imagined and so much more. She leaned in and trailed her tongue over his stomach muscles, then flicked it over the head of his shaft. He jerked beneath her tongue, a rough groan escaping his lips as he tightened his hold on her hair.

She felt like she'd been let loose in a candy store. Every delight she could imagine spread before her. And she wasn't planning on employing restraint.

She slipped her hand lower, took as much of him into her mouth as she could, reveling in the taste, the feel of him. She could feel the muscles in his thighs shaking, feel the tension in his body as he tried to maintain control.

She didn't want his control. She wanted him to lose it. She wanted him to lose it in a way that she couldn't. She wanted him to do it for her. She more than wanted it, she needed it. Needed his strength to dissolve beneath her, needed to be a part of his undoing. She wanted to exercise the power she had over him. And she did have it. She could feel it. Could feel just how close he was to losing it completely.

That was what she wanted. Needed. Craved. To have victory tonight, in his bed. To be perfection for him. For herself.

"Jessica," he said, and he tugged lightly, trying to move her away from him.

She didn't stop. She ran her tongue along his heavy length and she felt his ab muscles contract sharply beneath her hand.

"Jess," he said again. His tone a warning.

She lifted her head, her eyes locking with his. His gaze was clouded, sweat beaded on his forehead. A surge of power rushed through her. "This is for me," she said. "I want you like this. And I intend to have you."

She leaned in again and his fingers tightened, tangling deep in her hair, the slight sting of pain heightening the pleasure that created a hollow ache between her thighs.

A shaky laugh escaped his lips. "Doesn't it matter what I want?"

"Not in the least. But you like this, don't you?" She traced the head of his shaft with her tongue. "Don't you?"

"*Theos,* yes," he breathed his consent.

She continued to pleasure him with her lips and tongue. And she took everything. His ecstasy, every broken breath and trembling muscle, every curse, every word of praise.

This was her moment. Her pleasure. Her power.

Her taste of what she truly wanted. A hint of the feast she couldn't have.

She didn't stop until he found his pleasure, his body shaking, his skin slicked with sweat, every vestige of control stripped of him as he found his release.

He lay on his back after, stroking her cheek. She rested her head on his stomach and closed her eyes. Just for a moment.

She felt him stir beneath her. He sat up and brought her with him, kissing her on the lips. The kiss intensified, his tongue sweeping across her bottom lip, arousal pouring through her.

When she felt like she was on the edge, she pulled away. Her body trembled, her breath shaky and uneven. She had meant to push him to the brink. She hadn't realized that she would go with him. She needed sanctuary. Needed escape.

"That was it," she said, her voice choked. "I mean…I'm going back to bed now."

He frowned. "What do you mean 'that's it'?"

"Just what I said. Most men would be pretty happy with that."

His face was hidden in shadow, his tone dark. "Then why did you come to me tonight?"

"Because I wanted you. And I got to have you."

"You didn't have an orgasm," he said, his words blunt in the quiet of the room.

"I know, but that wasn't what I came for. I got to have a taste, no pun intended." She slid off the bed and crossed her arms beneath her breasts. "We can talk more tomorrow about how we're going to handle all this."

"This?" he said, indicating the bed.

She shook her head, heat prickling her cheeks. Not embarrassed heat, but anger. She was so mad at…everything. At her body, at Stavros, at herself. At the fear that lived inside of her. A tenant she couldn't seem to evict. "No. About Victoria and where we intend to go from here with that part of our arrangement. You wanted a night. This was a good night. Let's not ruin it now."

"I wanted more," he said. "I still want more."

She nodded. "I know." She wanted more, too. But any more would be far too much. She would have to be too vulnerable. She would have to give too much. Far more than she'd given tonight.

"Stay with me. Just sleep," he said.

That was tempting. Beyond. To sleep in his arms with her head on his chest. To listen to his breathing all night… it surpassed almost every other desire that lived in her.

Which meant she had to say no. "I need to go to bed."

His expression changed, hardened. "We'll talk tomorrow," he said.

"Okay."

She had a feeling that he wasn't going to stay on the topic she wanted to stay on. If there was one thing she'd learned about Stavros it was that beneath all that charm lay a stubbornness that rivaled her own.

Stavros's body still burned. It had been six hours since his late-night visit from Jessica and he couldn't get it, or her, out of his mind. The way she'd taken him, so confident, so bold and sexy. And the way she'd retreated, arms wrapped around her middle, looking like she wanted to disappear.

His feelings on the matter didn't make sense. He'd wanted her to stay. Even if it just meant holding her all night. He'd wanted…he wasn't sure what he'd wanted.

Her actions didn't make sense to him, either. Sex was all about pleasure and release, and she'd taken none for herself. She hadn't removed any of her clothes, he'd barely touched her, and yet, she'd acted as though it was what she wanted.

And then she'd acted like they weren't going to talk about it. She was so very wrong on that count.

His housekeeper refilled his mug of coffee and retreated from the terrace as he lifted the cup to his lips. There was another mug placed across from him and the contents were getting cold, but they were ready for Jessica, when she decided to show herself.

"Morning." He turned and saw Jessica, buttoned up into a yellow dress that covered her from knee to throat, a white belt spanning her tiny waist. She was clutching her little computer in her hands. Her tiny electronic shield.

"Good morning," he said, not bothering to be discreet in his appraisal of her. Her cheeks flushed as she sat down across from him.

She took a sip of her coffee and frowned, not swallowing, not spitting it back out, either.

"Cold?" he asked. She nodded, her frown intensifying. "Bitter?" She nodded again. A smile tugged at the corner of his mouth.

She swallowed slowly, her lip curling into a grimace. "I'll need fresh coffee."

"Leda will be back soon," he said.

"So, things went well last night?"

He said nothing, simply looked at her until the double meaning of her words hit her. He could tell when they did, because she blushed, her lips pulling into a pucker.

"With Victoria," she said sharply.

"Very well." He leaned back in his chair. His heart was beating faster than usual, and that surprised him. He was always in control of himself. Although, Jessica tested that, at every turn she did, and right in this moment, what he had to say to her made him feel…nervous. What her reaction might be made him nervous. "But there is a problem."

"What's that?"

"The same problem we discussed last night. I am currently…obsessed—" he hated the word, but it was the only one that fit "—with another woman, and I can't possibly get engaged to Victoria, much less marry her, while I'm still wrestling with it."

Her face paled, her green eyes looking more vivid set against waxen skin. "Me? This is me you're talking about? Good grief, Stavros, what does it take for a woman to scare you off?"

"A blow job at midnight might not be the best way to go about scaring a man off."

"Granted," she said tightly, some of her color returning.

"I did some reading on endometriosis last night."

Her mouth dropped open, a perfect, crimson O. "You did what?"

"I wanted to understand it more. To understand what you were telling me. I'm embarrassed to say I didn't know anything about it."

"I… Why should you?" The utter confusion on her face puzzled him.

"Because it…it seems like it's not uncommon and like I should. But now, I especially wanted to know about it because of you."

"I don't really have it anymore, like I said. At least I'm not symptomatic."

"You mentioned that, but you still don't want to have sex?"

"It's not that I don't want to. I do, I just…don't. I'm aware that that sounds stupid. But it's…complicated. It's wrapped up in a lot of little problems that you really don't want me to get into." Her green eyes chilled, hardened. "Like I said. I'm not fling material. Too many issues."

"It's understandable. But you also said you had a procedure that fixed most everything for you. Maybe it won't hurt now. Maybe…"

"You know, if it was only physical pain it wouldn't bother me. I've been through hell and back with physical pain. A little more would hardly wreck me. But the point is, I don't know if I can deal with that kind of relationship again. I don't know if I can deal with a man looking at me like I'm the living embodiment of his every crushed dream."

"Jessica, I am not your ex. I don't want anything from you but…"

"Sex. You want sex. And I suck at that, too. My own pain was offensive to him," she said, her words coming out harsh, bitter. "I just had to bite my lip and deal with it because it hurt his feelings. Because crying when it hurt made him feel bad. I had to hide anything I bled on because it disgusted him. And then even when I took steps to fix the pain, when I couldn't take it anymore, that was a failure in his eyes, too. I can't do this right now…"

Stavros felt sick. He pushed his coffee back into the middle of the table. "Tell me."

She looked away from him. "The bottom line is that he wanted kids, I can't have them."

She'd said as much last night. "I saw that endometriosis can effect fertility," he said.

A smile curved her lips. "Yes. It can. But not for everyone. And it doesn't mean it can't happen. But I can't. Because in order to try and fix my endometriosis, I opted to get a hysterectomy. He didn't want me to. He wanted to keep trying to conceive first and I…I couldn't take it anymore. In his mind, I gave up. Can't very well get pregnant if you haven't got an oven to put the bun in, right? To him, I gave up on kids. I gave up on us. I killed our dreams for my own comfort. I'm a selfish bitch. I told you that, remember?" She stood up. "Sorry. I have to go."

She turned and walked back into the house, her expression pale and set as marble. His stomach burned, acid, anger, eating away at him.

Not at her. Never at her.

He stood, and looked out at the ocean for a moment before walking back into the villa. He was more determined now than he'd been a few moments ago.

He needed Jessica. And she needed him. Even if it was only for a while, he was determined to have her. Determined to heal some of the wounds her husband had left behind.

Determined to have a stolen moment of time that belonged solely to him.

He had not been born to be the king. He had taken hold of it when it became clear that Xander would not. He had let go of so many things. So many desires he wouldn't let himself remember now. He had consigned himself to a marriage that was to be little more than a business arrangement.

He had given it all. Would continue to give it all for the

rest of his life. He would embrace the hollowness he had carved out inside of himself, let it fill with all the duty and honor he could possibly stand.

Just now, he was filled with Jessica. With whatever it was she made him feel. Something foreign, all-consuming. Something he wanted to embrace with a desperation he couldn't put into words.

For now, for just a little while, he would. If only she would allow it.

CHAPTER EIGHT

If POUNDING her head against a wall and repeating the "you are an idiot" mantra would have made any difference to the outcome of her morning conversation with Stavros, she would have done it. Unfortunately, no amount of self-recrimination would fix the fact that she'd vomited her emotional guts up for him to dissect whether he wanted to or not.

Yes, he'd asked. But he hadn't known what he was asking.

I did some research on endometriosis.

Replaying those words in her mind made her eyes sting, made her skin feel tight. When had anyone in her life done that for her? Her mother, her husband, her friends? When had anyone cared enough? Or been brave enough? As far as everyone in her life was concerned her condition only mattered in terms of how it affected them.

Only Stavros had asked. Only he had made that extra effort. Why? Why did he care for her at all? It didn't make sense.

The commanding knock on her door could only come from Stavros. She knew it by now.

"Come in," she said. There was no point in avoiding him. He wouldn't go away. He was like that.

The door opened and Stavros walked in, closing it behind him. "Why don't you let me decide what's too much work?"

She blinked. "What?"

"Can I be the one to decide if you're too much work? Because you keep telling me you are, and that I don't want to deal with you but...the thing is, I do."

He looked so sincere, so deadly serious, and she couldn't help but laugh. "Why? It doesn't make sense. Go...have a fling if that's what you need before you get married. There's a whole lot of women in bikinis down on the public beaches. Or hurry up and marry Victoria, so you can get to your wedding night. But why would you want to waste your time with me?"

"I want you. And if you don't want me, that's fine, but I'm pretty sure your actions last night mean that you do. So if you want me, take some time with me."

"I...I don't think I understand."

"Four weeks. Four weeks and I'll ask Victoria to marry me, and until then, I want you." He looked down. "I understand it's not the world's most romantic proposition, but it's all I can offer."

Her stomach seemed to be cold inside, and she knew that wasn't possible. "Yes, I know. I'm over twenty-eight, I can't have children, I probably have an annoying laugh. The reasons why I'm wrong for you are many and varied. Those are just the obvious ones."

"Yes," he said, the word flat, honest. "But that hasn't stopped me from wanting you."

"I...I don't know whether I'm flattered or insulted. Actually, scratch that, I don't know if I'm supposed to be flattered or insulted. I think I'm flattered, I'm just not certain I should be."

"Because it's a temporary offer?"

She lifted her thumb to her lips and gnawed the corner of her nail, nodding.

"I would never insult you by pretending I could offer something I couldn't. My responsibilities won't change. They are what they are. But I can't get you out of my head. I can't force myself to want Victoria when it's you that I see every time I close my eyes."

"No one's ever said things like this to me," she said, looking up at him, trying to see some hint in his expression that he was joking because...it didn't seem real.

"Not even your husband?"

"No. He uh...he was a college student when we got together. So was I. Young and stupid and very sincere, but not very poetic." She cleared her throat. "It didn't last, either, for all that we thought it would."

"Neither will this," he said.

She nodded. "But we won't pretend otherwise, will we?"

"No. I won't pretend with you, ever. Promise to do the same with me?"

"Yes," she whispered, not sure if she was agreeing to his last request, or his request for the four weeks. She was lost anyway. No matter how much she pretended she was undecided, she was lost to him. To her desire for him. Her curiosity. Yes, she was afraid, but she wanted him more than she wanted to keep hiding.

Because that's what it really was. She wasn't afraid of the pain of sex. She wasn't even as afraid of failing as she'd thought. She was more afraid that she would have sex, and that it would be good. And then she would lose her excuse to hold men at arm's length. She would lose that thing that kept her from seeking out another relationship.

She swallowed, trying to push her fear down. Fear she didn't want. Not now.

"I need you," he said, the words raw, lacking charm,

flirtation, any kind of artifice. "I'm not sure if you realize how much. I'm not sure you could, as it's something I don't entirely understand. But I need…you. This. I hope you want me."

She did understand. She needed him, too. As much as she needed to escape from the confines she'd put herself into, as much as she needed to move on. He felt like a necessity.

She hadn't ever thought of herself as a temporary kind of woman. But then, when sex was such an ordeal it was hard to think of it as something she might do recreationally. Still…Stavros made her want a taste of the illicit.

Of something she'd never really had, first because she'd met her husband at such a young age, and then because she'd developed endometriosis. And after that, because clinging to the past, wrapping herself in the memories of the pain, had become a shield against any sort of future hurt.

It also kept her tied to her old life. Tied to who she'd been.

She needed to be free of it. She finally felt ready to be free of it. It was all well and good to wish she could fully embrace her new reality. But she wasn't. And that was no one's fault but hers.

"Yes," she said again. "I want you, too. And now that you've given up on that fake flirting business I actually find you a lot more irresistible."

"What fake flirting business?"

"You know. That's not you, Stavros. This is. This is the man I can't resist."

He swallowed visibly, a muscle in his jaw twitching. "As long as you can't resist me."

"I could. But I'm not going to anymore."

He laughed, the sound as raw and ragged as his expression. "I couldn't resist you. That's why I'm here."

Her stomach contracted, her heart pounding faster. To

have such a big, strong man admitting he couldn't fight his attraction to her was…it was beyond her. And it restored something in her. Something she'd thought was so mangled beyond recognition it could never be fixed.

"This is stupid," she said, laughing, because if she didn't she thought she might cry.

"I know," he said, taking a step toward her, cupping her cheek in his palm. "I know." He rested his forehead against hers, his eyes closed.

She tilted her face and touched her lips to his, a gentle kiss, a question. One he answered with his own kiss, stronger, more certain. His tongue teased her, and she parted her mouth for him, sliding her tongue against his, the friction igniting a wave of heat in her stomach that spread to her breasts, down to her core.

"Wow. You really are an amazing kisser," she said, a shiver sliding down through her.

"And you are very honest."

She shook her head. "I'm not usually. I just do my very best to seem tough all the time and no one questions what I do or say too closely. They don't want me to kill them with snark. And that way I don't have to be honest. But for some reason, I am honest with you. I'm not sure why."

"You have the same effect on me," he said. "I can't fathom it."

"It's the lust thing. It's scrambling our brains."

A smile turned up the corners of his mouth. "Is that it?"

She nodded. "I'm not familiar with it on quite this level, but I remember feeling this way in college a couple of times."

"Yes, that sounds about right. You'd think at our age we would be impervious." He smiled slightly and it made her knees feel a little weak.

"Hey, watch it. No age jokes."

He kissed her again. "You are a beautiful woman. I cannot imagine you being any more attractive to me. Your dress today is lethal."

She looked down at her demure yellow dress. "This?"

"It has buttons," he growled. "And all I can think of is undoing all of those buttons."

Her face heated. "Really?"

"Oh, yes, really. I want to do it now, but I don't want to move too quickly."

"It's not even noon."

"So?"

"Isn't there a no-sex-before-noon rule?"

He laughed. "Sex isn't like alcohol. And if that's been your experience with it, I can tell you, you need your experience broadened."

She swallowed. "I'm a little nervous. A lot nervous." She wasn't sure what he would do to her, and that fear wasn't rooted in the fear of physical pain, but over how complete the loss of control might be. Over whether or not she would be able to hold onto her defenses.

He smoothed his thumb over her cheek. "Tell me, is there a specific act that causes worse pain?"

She nodded, finding that focusing on the physical was helpful. "Orgasm can cause pain, which…sucks." She breathed the last word with a shaky laugh. "The worst of it always came from…penetration. In the end at least."

He nodded slowly. "No sex. Not now. I want to take your dress off. I want to touch your breasts. Taste them, too. Nothing more. Nothing more until you're ready."

She could hardly breathe. His promises, so husky and sensual and perfect, had her body wound so tight she was certain she would break. "You really do have a way with words."

"Funny you should say that. My speechwriters usually

handle my words. I pride myself on being a man of action. What are words if you can't back them up?" He slid his hands down to the first button on her dress and slowly slid the little fabric-covered bead through the hole, letting the neck of the dress gap.

She wished she could capture the bravado she'd felt last night. But then, last night had been her game. She'd been in control, in her element. She'd been giving pleasure and feeding off of the residual. Here and now, Stavros had command of her. A reverse on last night, and she found she actually liked it.

He moved to the next button, then the next, pressing a kiss to her neck for each button. When he reached the button just beneath her breasts, he slid his tongue along the line of her collarbone, then down a fraction. He paused at her belt, sliding it through the buckle slowly, then letting it drop. He continued down, until her dress hung open, until his tongue was curving around the line of her bra, teasing her sensitive flesh.

She shivered as he pushed the dress from her shoulders and let it fall to the floor, leaving her in her white pumps and matching bra and panties.

"You are amazing," he said, dropping to his knees to press a kiss to her stomach. Tears filled her eyes and she couldn't stop them. She didn't want him to take her panties off, not this time. He would see her scars and she wasn't ready. Not yet.

She tugged on his shoulders, urging him up, and he complied, his hand on her back, toying with the catch on her bra, teasing them both. He took a step, his arms wrapped around her still. She stepped backward. They made a slow, smooth dance to the bed and he undid her bra as he laid her down, pulling it off and casting it aside.

He was half over her, his breathing harsh, his eyes on

her bare breasts. Thankfully, she knew they were one of her best features, so this was the easy part. It was made even easier when she caught the feral light in his dark eyes. "You are so much more beautiful than I imagined. Much more beautiful than I *could* have imagined. I have never seen a woman as exquisite as you." He cupped her, slid his fingers gently over her tightened nipples.

She arched into him, pleasure making her breath catch.

"Tell me if I do something you don't like," he said. "Tell me, and I'll stop."

She didn't want him to stop. Not ever. She reveled in his touch, in the feel of his rough, masculine hands on her tender skin. And when he replaced his fingers with his mouth, with the slick friction of his tongue, she felt a sharp tightening in her core, waves of pleasure, of pending release, rippling through her.

She gripped his hair, arched her body. She was close. She'd never been so close, so fast. She couldn't remember ever wanting anyone this badly, either.

"Oh, yes." She sighed, letting her head fall back.

He raised his head. "More?"

She nodded, biting her bottom lip. "Yes."

He moved his hand down her stomach and she was certain he would feel the line of scar tissue that ran just below the waistband of her underwear, but she was past caring. Past caring about anything. About the future. About possible pain. Even about the loss of control.

How could something that felt so amazing end in pain? Any kind of pain was worth it, surely.

He slipped his fingers beneath her panties, grazed the scar and continued down to where she was wet and ready for him. He teased the entrance to her body with his fingers, before sliding them over her clitoris. The sensation was like fire, burning heat from there throughout her body.

She gritted her teeth, her breath getting sharper, uneven. She curled her fingers into the sheets as he continued to touch her there. Soft, even strokes that brought her closer and closer to the edge.

He leaned in and kissed her mouth as he increased the pressure of his touch, and everything in her seemed to release at once, a flood of pleasure roaring through her, drowning out thought and sound. She cried out, not caring if she was loud, not caring that it was daylight, not caring that their relationship would only last a month.

Because there was nothing else. Not in that moment. There was Stavros. And there was what he made her feel.

Only when reality started piecing itself back together, did fear assault her. But there hadn't been any pain yet. Still, she waited. Waited for the low, dragging sensation that rivaled stories she'd heard about childbirth to begin.

And there was nothing. Nothing but a feeling of being replete. Nothing but a feeling of total bliss and satisfaction. She didn't feel as though she'd given her body away, didn't feel as though she was lost. She felt as though she'd gained a part of herself back.

A sob shook her body and she felt a tear slide down her cheek. The tears she couldn't find earlier. Tears she hadn't been able to find for a long time. Something in her shifted, changed. Like a dam had been broken inside of her, one she'd walled up to protect herself. One she felt she didn't need. Not now.

Stavros cupped her face, his expression fierce. "Did I hurt you?"

She bit her lip and shook her head. "No. You didn't. I can't...I can't remember the last time... Thank you."

He wrapped his arms around her and pulled her to him so that her head was rested on his chest. "Don't thank me.

I can't accept thanks for that. I took far too much pleasure from it for that."

"Realistically," she said, trying to escape from some of the moment's intimacy, impossible when she was mostly naked and cradled in his arms, but worth a try, "you have to see Victoria a couple more times before you propose."

He nodded. "All right."

"I know that will run during our…relationship. But I suppose as long as you don't…"

"I will be faithful to you, you don't have to worry about that. And I will be faithful when I am married," he said.

She swallowed. It was the right thing for him to say, the right thing for him to do. He should keep his vows. She believed in marriage, respected it. For all that she and Gil had screwed up their marriage, neither of them had cheated.

Still, a part of her died when he said it. "I'm glad. For all of that."

"This might not be the best idea. But I don't regret it."

"I can't, either," she said. It was the absolute truth. How could she regret what had passed between them? How could she regret the loss of a fear? There were others, of course. But she was free of one, too. And that wasn't a small thing.

"So, tell me," she said, attempting a subject change, in a bid keep things from getting too heavy, "what does a woman expect when she signs on to be your temporary companion?"

"I'm not sure. I've never had a relationship quite like this. Of course, I've never met a woman quite like you."

"What do you normally do?"

"There's that sort of coyness to it that one employs in a sexual relationships. Gifts, shallow conversation, references only to the here and now, nothing said of the future one way or the other. And with you, there's no coyness, that's for sure."

She smiled. "I don't do coy."

"I noticed." He tightened his hold on her. "All of my life has been devoted to fulfilling the needs of others. Right now, just now, I want to meet my own."

So this was for him, as much as for her. She liked knowing that. Felt empowered by it. Because there was something he needed to, and maybe she could provide it. Maybe she could be the one to give him moments of bliss. Moments that were purely his own, so that he would have the memories years later when his life was no longer his at all.

"What do you want?" she asked.

He sifted his fingers through her hair. "I want to sleep with you tonight. Just sleep, if that's all you want."

"That's too easy. What else?"

"To go to the beach. Which should be easy, since we're on an island. I am a man with the world at my fingertips in terms of the material. The thing I often find myself lacking in is a companion who makes life interesting. Who makes it fun. You be you, and I will simply enjoy it."

"Really, you're too nice. I feel outmatched."

"I like your prickles," he said. "Even more now that I understand them."

She sat up and wrapped her arms around herself. "I should get dressed."

"I'm in no hurry."

"I have some work to check on, just real quick, and then…and then we can do whatever we want. Because that's what we've decided to do, isn't it? Whatever we want for the next month."

He smiled at her and her heart felt like it tightened in on itself. She could do a month. A month was short enough. Short enough that he wouldn't start wishing she could be a million things she could never be.

CHAPTER NINE

Anything he wanted turned out to be much more low-key and much less in bed than she'd imagined it might be.

Stavros took her on a tour of the ruins just outside the city, and then down to the open-air markets to shop. The market ran just outside the boundaries of the packed harbor, small stalls crammed between buildings, the ocean just beyond them.

Stavros could have taken her anywhere in Piraeus. To the more modern quadrants of the city, to exclusive boutiques with cutting-edge fashion.

But he'd taken her here. Because he knew what she liked. He understood what she enjoyed. She did her best to ignore her constricted lungs and turn her focus to the items for sale.

There was an eclectic mix of trash and truly exquisite treasure on offer. Things she would have found at an average yard sale in her home town, fresh seafood and antiques all mingled together. She bought a necklace fashioned from fishing line and glass beads, and earrings made from old coins.

"It's certainly vintage," Stavros said, eyeing her purchases later at an outdoor restaurant.

"Yes, most definitely."

"You need a *pallas* to go with it."

She pulled her necklace out of the bag and held it up so

that the afternoon sun filtered through the glass beads. "All right, what's that?"

"The traditional draped dress. It would look beautiful on you."

"Not my typical style though, draped clothes."

"No. Not at all." Today she was in a full white skirt that went down past her knees and a red button-up top. All very crisp and tailored.

"It makes for an intriguing thought."

"Yes, but you don't like my clothes."

"No, I like your clothes very much, it's just that I find them a distraction. And now that I have permission to be distracted...well, I like them even more."

Her cheeks heated. He made her feel...he made her feel so new. Like this was fresh. Flirting, and eating together. The anticipation of sex. And she was anticipating it. Big-time. She smiled and looked down at her plate.

She ignored the little hint of fear that pooled in her stomach. If she felt so close to him now, what would happen after? She really hadn't ever been a fling girl. She'd been one and done. She'd met her husband right out of high school, and he was the man she'd married.

"What is it?" he asked.

"Nothing."

He reached over and took her chin between his thumb and forefinger, tilting her face up. "What?"

It was hard meeting his eyes. Intimate, suddenly. "I'm happy. I haven't...enjoyed anything like this in a long time."

"I haven't, either."

"Stavros, why is this marriage so important to you?" She wasn't sure where the question came from, only that it seemed essential, suddenly. "I mean, I know why you need to do it eventually. But it's more than that, I can tell. I just...want to know why."

He frowned. "I'm the only one, Jessica."

"I know."

"When Xander left, everything was chaos. My father was a wreck, my mother was gone. Eva was just a child. There was only me. My willingness to step in. I was a teenager, but just that show of strength and solidarity, and the years I spent after building up the economy, that made the difference. I need everything to be as it should be. I need it to have balance and order. I want it to."

"And Victoria will help with that."

"Victoria is only a piece of the puzzle. I've been setting all of this in place for years."

"I know," she said, looking away from him again. "Plans…I wish sometimes that some of mine had worked out. And sometimes…I'm glad they didn't."

Really, today was the first time she was honestly glad to be in a different place. With a different man. She hadn't loved her ex for years. But very often she'd longed to go back to a time when she did love him.

A time when her life had been full of possibilities. Instead of a time when so many of her dreams had died.

"Mine have to work out," he said. "For my people."

"Has Xander officially abdicated?"

"No. And he won't until after my father dies, which doesn't look like it will be soon. I am thankful for that."

"But you're playing chess," she said.

"What do you mean?"

"I actually suck at chess, but I have a brother who plays very well, and he used to talk me into playing when we were younger. I could never win, because I was always responding to his moves. He knew all of his moves from the beginning. And he had back-up maneuvers just in case I failed to be predictable, but mostly, he just followed the strategy he'd had since the opening move. You already know your checkmate."

He laughed and placed his hand over hers, his thumb blazing a trail of heat over her skin as he moved it back and forth. "But this is a move I did not see making."

"Do you regret it? Because we haven't done anything we can't take back."

He shook his head. "I don't. I should, I'm certain of that. This is unfair to you."

It was her turn to laugh. "How? I'm not some young, inexperienced girl. I've been married, I've been divorced. I've done love and loss. I'm a bit too cynical to get hurt by a temporary affair." She hoped that was true. She'd certainly believed it of herself before she'd met Stavros. Before she'd started caring for him.

How had that happened? He was so far removed from her. A prince, for heaven's sake. And a client. They shouldn't connect on any level. Yet, she felt like he was the one person who had a hope of understanding her. She felt she understood him. How had he started to matter so much?

He nodded. "I know. But your husband hurt you. I don't want any part of that. Of hurting you."

She forced out a laugh and lifted her wineglass to her lips. "By that logic, you should worry about yourself. Yes, he hurt me. But I hurt him, too. Marriage is a two-way street, and very rarely is everything the fault of one person. I'm capable of breaking a man's heart, Stavros, so perhaps it's me who should be giving you an out."

"I don't have a heart to break, Jess."

"I don't believe that."

"When have I had time to worry about my feelings? I have to take care of Kyonos. While my father took his rage and grief out on Xander, while Xander wallowed in his guilt, someone had to push it aside and stand up. I have made it my mission to never allow emotion to dictate what I do. It has no place in me." His eyes met hers, the blankness in them frightening. She was so used to his charming glimmer that seeing him now, flat, empty, made her feel cold. The problem was that it rang far truer than the charismatic charm ever had. As though this was really him. The real depth of him. "It is what I must do, to be the best king I can be. To be better than my father."

"I get that." If she hadn't been able to hide behind her wall of snark, she could never have done her job. Could never have gone on matching other couples, trying to help them find their happily ever after. She couldn't have done it if she'd allowed the wound from the loss of her own to keep on bleeding.

She'd learned to shut it off. To protect herself. That was all deserting her now.

Not the time.

The darkness in his eyes changed, warmed. "But for a while, I'm going to focus on this." He leaned over and pressed a light kiss to her lips. He'd barely touched her since their encounter in the morning, and it was so very welcome.

"I appreciate your focus," she said, her breath coming in shorter bursts now. She tried not to be so obvious, tried to regain control.

But she could tell, from the expression on Stavros's face, that he didn't have any more control than she did. And that made it all seem a little bit more acceptable. Made it feel better that she couldn't stop her stomach from fluttering and her heart from thundering, hard and fast.

Neither of them had command of the attraction. The fact she was a part of it, that she was able to drive a man to this point, it did wonders for her completely squished ego.

It affected more than that, but she didn't really want to ponder it on a deeper level.

"I can't focus on anything else when you're around," he said, sliding his fingers through her hair.

"It's hard to believe you needed my help finding a wife. You seem to have the romance thing down."

He shook his head. "Romance is an area I've always found myself lacking in. Not in seduction, or flirting, but that's a different matter, isn't it? It requires no sincerity. And the matter of my marriage…that's separate from either of those. You know that."

His eyes were intense on hers, desperation evident in their depths. Desperation for her to understand. She didn't know why, and she was willing to bet he didn't, either. Only that she felt it echo inside of her.

"I know," she said, covering his hand with hers. "But we aren't worrying about that, right?"

"I see you've finally gotten on board with the denial tactic."

"Reality has its place. But it's not here."

"Normally, I would disagree. I would disagree with the entire concept of this relationship. But I don't have the strength right now." The words were rough, a hard admission for a man who lived his life by his strength. Who had based every action on being stronger than those around him.

He was Atlas, with the world on his shoulders. Or at least a country.

He deserved to set it down for a second. To have some relief.

"The only reason you don't have the strength right now, is because you've had to be stronger than any man should have to be. You've given up too much." she said.

"Maybe. But until now I hadn't missed anything. But if I passed up the chance to be with you…I think I would miss it for all of my life."

His words hung between them, thick and serious. And

far too true. They'd always spoken with honesty, it seemed like they couldn't help speaking with honesty. But this was a hard truth to take. Mostly because it was true for her, too, and admitting he was that important, that essential, scared her.

She swallowed, blinking to try and dispel the stinging in her eyes. "I would certainly hate to miss this." She looked at the view, at the sun glinting off the crystalline water. It was easy to look at the scenery and say it. Easy to let him think she might mean something else.

Far too difficult for her to let herself be vulnerable to him. To let him know how much he was starting to mean to her. It was almost harder to admit to herself how much he was starting to mean to her. Because she was tired of wanting the impossible.

"Jess." He whispered her name and he turned to look at him. His expression stopped her heart. He looked so hungry, so sad. And just as quickly as the emotions became evident on his face, they disappeared. "I do have some work to complete today, and then I would like to see you again. After dinner?"

She nodded. "Yes." She was grateful for a break, a reprieve. Because her chest felt so tight, far too tight, and she was finding it difficult to breathe.

This was supposed to be about her. About reclaiming a part of herself she thought was lost. About letting go of her past, not clinging to someone else. And she couldn't lie and say Stavros meant nothing to her. Of course he did. She liked him. She wanted him to have this, this last thing that he desired, before he gave himself over to his country.

But she was going to try to lie and say that was the end of it. She was going to try and do that for as long as she could.

She would use the time apart to try and get a grip on the other emotions, the unwelcome ones.

"Then I'll see you back to the villa."

She nodded, trying to ignore the fullness inside of her that was keeping her lungs from expanding all the way. "That sounds good."

Yes, she needed to get a grip, and she needed to get it badly.

She'd gone into her marriage a naive idiot, and she'd learned a lot about the reality of life since then. That, coupled with the fact that she knew her relationship with Stavros wouldn't last, should be enough to keep her head on straight.

Sadly, she wasn't certain it was.

"Jessica?" The villa was empty when Stavros returned later that evening. It was later than he'd intended. Mainly because he'd spent the evening sitting in his Piraeus office, staring out at the ocean and trying to get a grip on his rioting libido.

And the strange twinge in his heart that seemed to hit him hard and radiate down to his stomach whenever he pictured Jessica's face.

He was much later than he should have been, and he half expected her to be in bed. He prowled the halls for a few moments, opened the door to her room and confirmed that it was empty. He'd known right away.

He could feel that she wasn't here. A strange sensation, an impossible one, and yet, he had complete certainty in it. Strange how she'd done that. How she'd opened him back up to feeling.

Stranger that he wasn't fighting it.

Just for this month. Just a little while.

He walked out onto the terrace and looked down at the beach below. He could see her by the shore, her silhouette outlined by the silver moon. He walked down the terrace stairs, and out to the beach, pulling the knot on his tie and letting it fall somewhere in the sand. He discarded his jacket and kept moving to her.

No matter where she was, he felt compelled to find her. To go to her. He could feel her absence nearly as keenly as he could feel her presence. And he wasn't certain what that meant. Only that he had to be near her. And that if the force of his physical desire weren't so powerful, weren't so all-consuming, the need that came with it, the need to be with her, would be frightening. At least with the lust there, he had something else to focus on. Something to take the edge off the unfiltered emotion she called up in him with so much ease.

He walked soundlessly on the sand, discarding his shoes, not caring about their fate. Jessica turned sharply, and he wondered if she could feel him, too.

"Hi," she said, her voice barely audible above the sound of the waves on the shore.

"Sorry I'm late."

"You didn't give me a time. It's okay."

"Still, it's pretty late."

She shrugged. "It's okay. I had a nice evening. I called Victoria and told her to expect an invitation to an event in Kyonos. I hope that was okay."

"It was the right thing to do. No matter how I feel about it."

"It's not exactly ignoring it, I admit. But we both know you can't just not contact her at all over the next month."

His stomach tightened. "I know."

"Don't you have a celebration ball coming up for when Eva and Makhail return from their honeymoon? It's on the copy of your schedule I received and I thought it would be the perfect opportunity for you to be seen with Victoria."

"Oh, yes. I had forgotten."

"She should go to that. With you. Give a hint as to your

developing relationship. That way your people can really look forward to the engagement announcement."

His people. That was what all of this was about. His country. His heart. He had thrown himself into it, completely, into planning what he would do to make it better, to heal it. And that was why he was marrying Victoria.

He couldn't lose sight of it. But it was so easy to do when Jessica filled his vision. So easy to simply let his desire for her color everything. That was emotion. That was weakness. He could not afford it.

Just right now, it was okay though. Just for this moment in time. He moved to her, unable to stand apart from her any longer. Unable to be so close yet not touching her.

He sifted his fingers through silken strands of blond hair. "I missed you," he said. He wasn't sure why he said it, even though it was true.

He wasn't certain that level of honesty had a place in their arrangement. But he wasn't sure what else he should say, either. Wasn't sure what to hold back and what to give.

Holding anything back when Jessica was around seemed an impossibility. He wasn't sure he wanted to, and that was a new feeling entirely.

Lust he'd dealt with. He'd put it aside when he had to, embraced it when it was convenient. He'd never been controlled by it. But it had never before been accompanied by this strange…ache. An ache that seemed to spread through his body, sink down deep into his bones, beyond, down into his soul.

Wanting Jessica was painful. And it was more real than anything in his recent memory. He craved it. Because it was better than not being near her. Than not wanting her. He wasn't sure what kind of madness it was, only that for now he wanted to drink it in.

"Jessica, I want to kiss you."

She nodded, her gaze level with his. "I'm game. I like it when you kiss me." She had a bit of her false bravado in place, but it was all right. One of them needed to keep their guard up, and he wasn't certain he could.

When his mother had died, he had been the only one to hold himself together. He had been the one to pick up and move forward. He hadn't been allowed to grieve. Hadn't had time to feel. He had closed down.

But he couldn't shut these feelings off. Couldn't staunch the flow of emotion that seemed to bleed inside of him like a hidden wound. When he looked at Jessica, he had no control.

"I want to do more than that. I want to make love with you tonight. But you tell me, if it hurts. And I'll stop. I don't care how hard it is for me to stop, I will. I would never hurt you." Even as he said the words he feared they weren't true. Not that he wouldn't stop making love with her if it hurt, he was confident he would do that.

But he feared he might hurt her emotionally. That he might have a part in causing her further pain that way. He didn't want to, but to avoid it he would have to turn back. And at this point, even that would hurt her.

More than that, he feared what would happen to himself. Selfish, maybe. But he felt like he was standing at the edge of a fire, toying with the idea of touching the flame. Then throwing himself into it.

They were in too deep to escape unscathed. But then, maybe they had been from the beginning. That connection—instant, seemingly physical—had been more from the moment they'd met.

She nodded slowly. "I want that. And I'm not even nervous. Which is crazy but I just…know it will be good. That I'll be good."

"Something I have no doubt about," he said, forcing words through his tightened throat.

She laughed. "I'm glad."

"Oh, Jess, you are the most beautiful woman. The most fascinating. Bewitching." He kissed her. Her lips were so soft, so warm. They heated him, all the way through his body, his blood burning in his veins, his body getting hard.

She parted her lips and angled her head, her hand pressed to his cheek. He took advantage of the move and slid his tongue into her mouth, sliding it against hers, the intimate action sending a hard kick of lust through him.

It roared in him like a beast, one that demanded satisfaction. That demanded he lay her down in the sand and take what he needed. That he use her to fill the emptiness inside of him. Because she could. She was the only one who could.

He put his hands on her hips, braced her. Braced him. He curled his fingers in, gripped the full skirt of her dress tightly in his palms. He wouldn't do that to her. He wouldn't make this hard and fast, he wouldn't make it about his satisfaction.

He would give to her. He would control his own need. He would master it.

It was Jessica who changed the game. Jessica who moved her hands over his chest, down to where he was hard and ready for her. She was a mass of contradictions, his Jessica. So confident in giving pleasure. So hesitant to receive it.

So afraid to release control.

She cupped him and he nearly lost his head then and there, her palm sweet and knowing on his erection, sliding over the length of him.

"Oh, yes," she whispered against his lips. "I'm so ready for this."

He took her hand and moved it away from him, his body

protesting. He lifted it to his lips and kissed her palm. "Not like that, Jess. Not this time."

"Stavros…"

"You aren't in charge. I know you don't like to hear that. But that's the way it's going to be."

Her eyes rounded and he wondered if he'd taken her a step to far. But she didn't move away. She moistened her lips and slid her hand around to the back of his neck, her fingers sifting through his hair. She kissed his jaw, his ear.

He chuckled when he felt her teeth scrape against his earlobe. "I see how it's going to be," he said.

"Do you?" she said, her voice trembling, betraying a hint of nerves.

"Well, that isn't entirely true. I can't really guess how it's going to be. Because I have never felt this way about a woman before." As he said it, he realized how true it was. "I have never wanted a woman as I want you."

"Glad we're on the same page there. I've never felt like this, either, not even before…not even before…not ever."

"Then we're both equal. And for that I'm glad. I would hate to be standing here, ready to lose my mind with wanting you, with you feeling completely calm and certain."

"Oh, no sweat there, Stavros. I'm shaking," she whispered.

He swore. "Sorry, I'm losing my finesse."

"Good. I don't need your finesse. You're a very charming man, Stavros, and you seem to come by it effortlessly, no matter how you really feel. I would much rather have something real."

"You have it." He kissed her again, through with talking. Words were too difficult now. He just had to show her. Because it was the absolute truth. With her there was no artifice. He had tried to put distance between them with his charming persona, and he hadn't been able to. She made him real.

She made him real in a way he could never remember being before.

He wrapped his arms around her and pulled her flush against his body, sighing when her full breasts made contact with his chest. She was soft and perfect, everything a woman should be. He ran his hands over her curves, the indent of her waist, the fullness of her hips, the round curve of her butt. He palmed her, his body shuddering.

"Buttons," he growled, taking his hands from her backside and turning his focus to the front of her dress. Most of her dresses had buttons, but he was half convinced she'd chosen this one to torment him thanks to his earlier comments.

Her wicked smile confirmed it. He moved slowly, pushing each button through the hole at half the speed he could have done it in. Teasing them both. It was worth it. She bit her lip and watched him work. Even in the dim light, he could see the color mounting in her cheeks. He could feel her breath shorten, her breasts rising up against his fingers as he worked at the buttons there.

He was hard, burning with the need to take her, to join with her.

He pushed the top of the dress down, letting it fall around her waist. She had a lace bra on beneath it, thin and sexy. He slid his thumb over one breast, felt her nipple harden beneath his touch.

He moved to the next set of buttons on until the skirt loosened enough to fall down her hips and pool in the sand.

She was barefoot already, and now she was wearing nothing more than a pair of lace underwear and bra. He'd had her this undressed before, but not all the way. He unhooked her bra in one deft movement and consigned it to the sand with the dress.

"You're perfection," he said, cupping her breasts, teasing her nipples. She closed her eyes, her lips parted slightly. He took advantage of the moment and kissed her, then moved to her neck, her collarbone, before drawing one tightened bud between his lips and sliding his tongue over it. "And you taste amazing," he said.

She shivered beneath him, and he felt an answering tremor echo in his own body. He'd never felt so connected to a lover before. He'd always been committed to giving pleasure, because sex was only satisfying if all involved got what they needed. But he'd never felt dependent on his partner's response. Had never needed to draw the pleasure out like this, to be sure it was superior to his own. To be sure it was superior to any she'd had before.

He got on his knees in the sand, not caring about his suit, not caring about anything but the need to taste her everywhere. He slid his tongue along the waistband of her panties and he felt her stiffen.

"Come on now, Jessica, don't get shy on me."

She gripped his shoulders, the cold from her fingertips seeping through his shirt. She didn't stop him. He hooked his fingers into the sides of her underwear and tugged them down her legs.

She stepped out of them, her movements unsteady. He looked up at her and saw a shimmer of tears in her eyes. When he looked back down, it wasn't simply the gorgeous triangle of curls at the apex of her thighs that caught his attention. It was the scar that ran just above it. A thin line, an imperfection that meant very little to him in terms of how it looked.

But one he knew held a wealth of pain. Her pain. He could not remain unaffected by that. He was grateful he was on his knees, because the hard punch it delivered to his stomach might have taken him there had he not been down already.

He could hear her teeth chattering. "Stavros…"

"Oh, Jess." He leaned in and pressed his face to her stomach, kissing her there, just beneath her belly button. "You are amazing to me."

He lowered his head and traced the same line the surgeon's knife had followed, pressing kisses to the depressed section of skin. He didn't give her a chance to protest. He moved lower and flicked the tip of his tongue over her clitoris. A raw sound escaped her lips and she clung more tightly to him, her nails digging sharply into his shoulders.

He held her hips tightly and continued his exploration of her body with his lips and tongue. He could feel her shaking beneath his touch, and that was good, because he was shaking, too. He couldn't remember wanting a woman more, couldn't remember if the taste of woman had ever been essential. He was certain it never had been before.

Jessica was utterly unique. Comparing her to other experiences, comparing this moment to other experiences, was an impossibility.

He slipped his hand between her thighs and pressed a finger slowly inside her body, she froze for a moment, her hands gripping at his shirt and he felt her muscles contract around him as she found her release. It was her orgasm, her pleasure, and yet he felt spent. Satisfied.

But still in need of more. He was so hard his body burned.

She slid down to her knees, kissing him, her body pressed against him, her hands tearing at the buttons on his shirt. He was sure more than one was made a casualty in her haste, but he didn't care. Nothing mattered now. Nothing but being joined to Jessica. Nothing but finding some solace from the ache. From the emptiness he'd never been cognizant of until she'd walked into his life.

He helped her with his pants, shucking them off as quickly as possible. She pressed lightly on his shoulders, pushing him back into the sand. She slid her hands down his chest, his torso, along the side of his erection, teasing but not touching.

"Careful," he groaned.

She smiled, a sassy, sleepy smile of a woman who'd been satisfied, but who was still hungry for more. The big difference between the two of them right now was that she'd had the edge taken off, and she had the time to tease. He feared he did not.

She moved over him, and he put his hands on her waist, tilting his face up to pull one nipple into his mouth. She arched into him and he slid one hand down her back, guiding her so that his erection was pressing against her slick entrance.

"It's up to you now," he said, words nearly impossible to force through his tightened throat.

She bit her lip, her eyes on his. He could see her fear and he wished there was something he could to ease it. He kept his hold on her steady, kept his body still, gave the control back to her. He didn't want to move too quickly, didn't want to do anything to ruin the moment.

She lowered herself onto him, taking him inside an inch at a time. It took all of his strength not to thrust up into her. He kept his focus on her face. Her lips parted, her expression intense. And when she had him inside all the way, she let her head fall back, a slow breath escaping her lips.

"Oh, yes," she whispered.

"Good?" he asked.

She looked down at him, a smile touching her lips. "So good. And not enough."

She tilted her hips and pleasure flashed through him like a flood, pouring over him, taking over him. She set the pace, but he moved with her, thrusting up into her body, encouraged by the sounds of ecstasy coming from her lips. She planted her hands on his chest, her face tilted down, her hair covering them both, shielding them.

He could feel his orgasm building, taking him to the edge. He clung to it, every ounce of his willpower channeled into keeping his control. He had to give her more. One more. One more graceful movement and she tossed her head back, her breasts thrust forward. He captured one with his lips and she froze, her mouth open on a silent scream.

And then he let go. He was falling, lost, unsure if he would ever come back to earth. Back to himself. But Jessica was there. And that meant nothing else mattered. Nothing but the pleasure that bound them together, nothing but the all-consuming sensation that was washing over him like a wave, drawing him farther and farther away from shore.

She collapsed over his chest, her breath hot on his skin, her breasts pressed against his stomach. He wrapped his arms around her and smoothed his hand over her hair.

He could feel her tears on him, dampening his skin. "Jess…don't cry."

"It's good crying," she said, sniffing.

"No pain?"

She shook her head. "No pain. You're amazing, by the way."

"That was all you."

"I don't think so," she said. "It's never been quite like that for me before."

He wound a silken strand of her hair around his finger, then released it, watching as the ocean breeze caught it. "Well, it hasn't ever been quite like that for me, either."

"You've never had to deal with a neurotic woman who had mass amounts of sexual hang-ups and cried afterward?"

He laughed, so strange because he had her naked body pressed to his front and he was becoming increasingly aware of the sticky, itchy sand at his back. And he couldn't remember ever wanting to laugh after sex. Sleep. Go back to his own bed, yes. But not laugh.

He sat up and brought her with him, holding her on his lap. "You are truly unique." He kissed her, drank her in. Would he ever feel like he wasn't starving for her?

He stood and swept her into his arms, looking out at the waves, the breeze warm on his bare skin. "Hang on," he said.

He ran toward the water and she tightened her hold around his neck, making a sharp, squeaking sound as they hit the waves, the water spraying around them. He walked out into the surf and spun them around. He set her down gently, the water lapping around her hips. She was laughing, breathless. He was shocked to discover that he was laughing and breathless, too.

She didn't just make him feel. She made him feel everything. All at once. And in such a big way he was sure he would burst with it.

"You're crazy," she said, kissing his mouth, her lips tasting of salt water and Jessica.

"Maybe a little." He looked at her face, so pale and lovely in the moonlight. "Yeah, maybe a little." He couldn't stop the smile from spreading over his face, couldn't fight against the strange, expanding feeling in his chest.

She wrapped her arms around his waist. "You're like Prince Charming's hot cousin. Prince Sexy."

"No nicknames," he said.

She laughed against his chest. "All right, fine. No nicknames." She smoothed her hands over his back. "You've got sand all over your back, Prince Sexy."

"I wonder whose fault that is?"

She looked up at him, the expression on her face impish. "No clue."

Something in his chest seemed to break, causing a release. Like a bird escaping the confines of a cage. A strange sensation assaulted him. Happiness. Freedom. Things he didn't have a lot of experience with.

If only he could hold on to it forever.

This month would have to do. Four weeks to carry him through the rest of his life.

CHAPTER TEN

"Stay in bed with me tonight." Stavros tightened his hold on her hand when they reached the top of the stairs back at the villa.

"You want me to sleep with you?"

"Eventually." A wicked smile spread over his lips and her heart expanded. Sex, lovemaking, whatever it had been, with him was like a whole new experience.

She should feel…some sort of awkwardness. It was their first time together after all. Walking back from the beach with him completely naked, her beautiful 1950s-secretary dress discarded and uncared for, should have left her blushing.

The memory of what it had been like to ride him, to be filled with him, to lose her mind completely when she orgasmed, rushed over her. How vocal she'd been both when he'd gone down on her and when he'd been in her, should have made her want to hide under the covers.

But she felt…surprisingly relaxed. And also still turned on.

She'd never experienced this sort of comfort in her own skin before. Even when she'd been younger with nothing medically wrong with her, she'd had insecurities. Her hips were a little wide for her body, her stomach not perfectly flat.

It had taken her a long time to let Gil make love with her with the lights on. And earlier she'd let Stavros touch her with the sunlight filtering through the window. Maybe it was her age. Maybe she'd finally hit that point where she just didn't care. With Gil she'd been an eighteen-year-old virgin, after all. A couple years later and they'd gotten married. Then things had started going wrong with her body.

And now things were so much better. The sex had been so good she didn't think she could have felt anything but good about it if she'd tried. His pleasure had been obvious. He'd had no insecurities, no anger to project onto her. And she'd just basked in her own pleasure, in the way they'd been connected, like one person. She hadn't had to wonder if she'd been right, because she could feel that she had been. That they'd been in perfect sync.

And that was a new experience. She didn't feel like there were ghosts hovering in the background anymore. She hadn't realized how much of herself had still be wrapped up in things from the past. How afraid she'd been of letting it go. Because clinging to it had been less scary than moving on.

"I just want you to know, that really was the best ever," she said.

He smiled. "You're very good for my ego."

"As if your ego needed inflating."

"It may not have needed it. At least not from just any woman. From you it means a lot more than that. So much more than empty flattery."

She cleared her throat, tried to deny the tender feelings that were swirling in her stomach. "I'm definitely staying in your bed tonight."

"Good." They walked down the hall hand in hand and he pushed the door open to his room, scooping her into his arms again as he had at the beach. "Shower first though. I'm still sandy."

He carried her into the bathroom and set her down on the bright white marble floor before turning on the water in the shower.

She turned and caught her reflection in the mirror. There were red splotches on her body, from sand and Stavros's whiskers. Her cheeks were pink from the sun, her hair tumbled beyond reason, stringy from the salt water. Her scar was still there. Still impossible to ignore.

But her eyes…they looked so happy.

She lowered her hand and ran her fingertips across the line that ran below her belly button.

"It's nothing to worry about," he said, wrapping his arms around her from behind and lowering her hand. "You're beautiful."

"Do you know…you're the first person besides my doctor to see me since I've had that scar."

"I didn't know," he said.

"Well, that was… This," she said, moving her hand back to the scar, "was the end of my marriage."

"He divorced you because you got a hysterectomy?"

She but her lip and shook her head. "No. I divorced him after he wouldn't come to the hospital to see me. To sit with me. After I came home and all he would do was look at me like…like I'd betrayed him."

"Bastard."

She shook her head. "I don't know. Maybe not. Maybe… maybe I did the wrong thing. Maybe if we would have kept trying it would have worked. Maybe the first four years of trying weren't enough. Maybe if there would have been four more years, or IVF or something…it would have worked. I was the one who couldn't take it anymore. My doctor told me the hysterectomy would make my pain go away and so I jumped at the chance."

"What about adoption? Why wouldn't he adopt a child?"

She swallowed. "It wasn't the same to him. It...wasn't what he wanted." She would have done it. Gladly. Happily.

"Jessica—" he turned her so that she was facing him "—how can you think you made a bad decision? And what business did he have making you feel bad for dealing with pain the way you had to? It wasn't his pain. It wasn't his right to make the decision. You said yourself he did his best to ignore your pain. It wasn't his right to make you suffer for trying to make it stop."

"Sometimes I think so, too," she said, her voice breaking. "A lot of the time I do. For the last couple months before the procedure I was on a steady pain-pill diet. That made me feel a bit happier, but it also made me sleepy. Made my brain foggy and made me unable to do my job."

"That's unacceptable. I can't believe you were in so much pain. I can't believe he didn't care." He shook his head. "That's too much," he said, his voice rough.

"I know," she whispered. "And he never...he never wanted to know how bad it was. He just didn't...he didn't want things to change. He didn't want a sick wife that couldn't stand to be touched. Didn't want a woman who was broken. It wasn't what he signed on for."

"He *never* asked you how badly you hurt?" Stavros touched her cheek. "He didn't care?"

"I don't know. I don't...I was so convinced he loved me. He was my husband. But on this side of it, I get angry. I wonder how you could watch someone suffer and only care about how it made you feel. I... And he said I was a bitch. But I wasn't." Her voice caught a sob sticking in her chest. "I wasn't. He was a bastard. And he didn't love me.

He didn't even have the decency to divorce me. He made me do it so he could hate me for that, too."

"And you did what you had to do. For yourself. And it was right. You know that, don't you?" His expression was so earnest, so impossibly sincere. It made her heart ache.

"I do. But then sometimes I think I gave up too quickly." *I would be a mother.* Her own words echoed in her head. "I'll never know if I could have conceived if…"

"And then you would have stayed with a man who loved the ideal better than he loved you. You don't deserve that."

She laughed. "Funny you should say that. About the ideal. I always think his new wife looks too much like me for comfort."

"He's remarried?"

"Yes. And they have a baby. The sad part? I cried for two days when I found out she was pregnant. I hated her. I hated her so much. And that was so stupid. So wrong."

He shook his head. "Not wrong. You're human."

"Yeah. I am. Too human. But you're right. I do deserve better than him. Better than being the vehicle for his dreams. Better than being his failed dream. He was able to move on and have the exact same thing. I can't. I am who I am. I have the body I have."

"You say that, that you can't leave yourself, but that he can move on, but you overlook something."

"What?" she whispered.

He cupped her face, his thumbs moving over her cheekbones. "He can't leave himself. He's a sad, selfish person. And that's who he is. He won't grow or change. He'll never understand what he lost. His punishment is living with himself. And living without you."

"Oh," she breathed, words failing her completely.

"Come here." He took her hand and led her into the shower. His hands slid over her curves, the water making his touch slick. It wasn't sexual, even though it did arouse her. His touch was comforting.

She had him turn around so she could rinse the sand from his skin. Kiss the place a rock had bit into his flesh while they'd made love. They helped dry each other off, and then they got into bed.

He pulled her against the curve of his body, his arms so strong, his heat warming her.

It was so intimate. It felt far more intimate than anything she'd ever experienced. Because for the first time she felt like the man in her bed understood her. That there wasn't a secret thought in her mind she knew he wouldn't approve of.

Stavros felt like her ally. Sadly, most of the time her husband had felt like an enemy.

Her pain had caused him pain, so he hadn't allowed her to talk about it. Her escape from pain had been unacceptable to him, so he hadn't supported it. His words had wounded her. Flayed the skin from her bones.

But Stavros's words were healing.

"He really let you go through that by yourself?" His fingers grazed her scar.

"Yes. He didn't want me to do it."

He swore, a truly foul word in Greek that she knew roughly translated to something that would be physically impossible for her ex to do to himself. She laughed. "I appreciate how strongly you feel about it. But I've been my own champion for long enough that I don't need your anger." Was it so wrong that she wanted it? That it soothed her?

He turned her so she was facing him. "I need to be angry at him. For me."

Her throat tightened and tears stung her eyes. "Oh."

"He should have been there for you."

"He couldn't do it. He couldn't stand that I was killing our dreams. And without those dreams…there was no point."

"I don't believe that, Jess. You're enough to fulfill a man's dreams all on your own."

His words hung between them. She couldn't speak. She didn't bother to wipe away the tears that were falling down her cheeks. Tears it felt so good to finally be able to cry.

When Stavros woke up the next morning, Jessica was lying across the end of the bed, playing a game on her iPad. Her lips were pursed in concentration, her focus on the screen. She must have gone back to her room to get both the computer and a set of pajamas that consisted of a thin T-shirt and some very short shorts.

But she'd come back to his room. That thought brought him more pleasure than it ought to. "What are you doing?" He sat up and leaned over to get a good view of the screen.

"Oh." She turned and looked at him, the impact of her smile carrying all the force of a prize fighter's right hook. "Waiting for you to wake up."

"How do you play the game?"

"You shoot these little birds out of the slingshot and try to hit the pigs." She demonstrated by drawing one slender finger over the touch screen and aiming her feathered bullet at its target. "Yes!" She sat up after she hit her target, pumping her fist.

He laughed, this moment, this one where she was so happy, so relaxed, where he felt the same things, was one he would cling to always. One he would hold inside of him to keep. To treasure.

You are weak. You find it too easy to grow attached to this woman.

He had always feared as much. That he was as weak, as

governed by his emotions as his father, as his brother. That it would be his ruin, the ruin of his country.

But he didn't see how it could be. Looking at Jessica now, being with her, he felt strong. Stronger than he had in his life. More vulnerable in some ways too, but he wondered if it was good.

Then he wondered about his sanity.

"High score!" she said.

He smiled. "Don't you do a dance when you get high scores?"

She treated him to a bland look. "I told you, you don't get to see my dance."

"So, I can see you naked, but I can't see you dance?"

She stood on the bed and looked over her shoulder. "Don't tell anyone about this."

"I wouldn't dare."

She swayed her hips from side to side, her arms moving in time, her lips pulled to the left. She twirled in a circle, continuing in the same motion. He felt, for a moment, like he was watching himself from a distant place. An observer rather than a participant. Like it couldn't be real. This snatch of happiness, this moment of pure connection and silliness with another person. He had never felt anything like it.

His heart seemed to draw tight around itself and squeeze hard. The same heart he had professed not to have.

She plopped back down onto her knees in front of him. "There. Now I've done it."

He leaned in and kissed her. "Amazing."

She was amazing. What she made him feel was amazing. He felt different. He wanted to fight against it. He wanted to embrace it, and all the changes he could feel her making inside of him.

Just take this time. Just this time.

He put everything into the kiss, into losing himself in it. In her.

For once, he didn't want to think. He only wanted to feel.

They spent the next week in Greece. Jessica handled clients remotely, and Stavros went to work in the city, or worked from his office in the villa. And mostly they had a lot of sex.

Jessica was pretty sure she had a perma-grin from all the ecstasy she'd been exposed to over the past seven days. She was a little worried, though, because she didn't seem to be getting tired of him. Worse, she missed him a lot when he was working, or when she was working. And if he got up to work on his computer at night, she would wake up, feeling his absence almost immediately.

She'd been sleeping in her own bed since well before her divorce, but it had been so easy to get used to having someone again. No, not just someone. Because even after eight years of sharing a bed with Gil he hogged the covers and pushed her to the edge of the bed.

Stavros hogged the covers sometimes. And he certainly took up more than his half of the king-size bed. But she was content to curl around him and let him hold her. And she didn't really mind that he kept most of the blankets. Because she liked having him there. Liked waking up and seeing his face first thing. Liked having him be the last thing she saw before she went to sleep.

That was a bit of a problem. Because this was temporary. They had three weeks left.

That sucked big-time.

They were also going to have to figure out how to make it work in Kyonos, which would be its own problem.

She walked into Stavros's—now their—bedroom just in time to see him walking out of the bathroom with a white towel slung low on his lean hips, his muscles shifting pleasantly as he ran his fingers through his dark, damp hair.

"Hey, stranger," she said.

He turned and looked at her, his smile making her heart stop beating for a moment. "Did you get any work done?"

"Uh…yeah. I had a woman from India contact me. She's from a very wealthy family and she wants to use my contacts to find someone better than the guy her parents are pushing her toward. She seems fun. I'm looking forward to it."

She was looking forward to matching anyone except Stavros, really.

"You sound excited."

"I am."

"I understand if you have to travel once we're back in Kyonos," he said. "If you need to go and meet this client."

"I probably will." She didn't really like to think about it. To consider wasting nights away from him when their time was already so limited.

"You can use my plane."

"Oh, no, I don't want to do that."

He put his hands on his hips and her eyes were drawn to the cut lines that ran down beneath the towel, an arrow to an even more interesting part of his anatomy. "Jessica, don't be difficult."

Annoyance coursed through her, battling against the arousal being near him all damp, fresh and half-naked had caused. "Tough luck, Prince Sexy, I am difficult, if you hadn't noticed. And I'm not going to take advantage of you. My expenses are all worked into the fees I charge my clients. I'm a businesswoman. A very successful one. Maybe not quite on your level, but I do very well for myself."

"I know that. But if you use airports, it will all take longer. I can have you flown any time, day or night, in superior comfort in half the time."

"Well. Yes. But still, it's not my plane."

"Then I'll sell you a ticket."

She narrowed her eyes. "For?"

"If I say sexual favors will you knee me in the groin?"

She bit the inside of her cheek to keep from smiling and offered him a deadly glare. "Yes."

He named an insultingly low figure.

"No dice," she said. "I'll be flying out of Kyonos International. Deal with it."

He reached out and grabbed her around the waist and tugged her to him. "You are a pain."

"Yeah, so? You like it." She grabbed his towel and tugged it, letting it fall to his feet.

He smiled down at her, then kissed her nose. "Maybe."

"What time are we headed back to Kyonos?"

"This afternoon." His tone said what his words didn't. That it was too soon. That even though they still had time together, the real world would be intruding. That he didn't want that.

She didn't, either. She wanted to freeze time and live in the bubble for a while. Where reality wasn't such an intrusive force. Where chemistry was enough of a reason to be with someone. Where her ability to produce children, to be a figurehead and not just be Jessica, wouldn't be essential to her being with Stavros.

But that wasn't real. That couldn't last. And they both just had to buck up and deal with it.

"All right. I guess I should get packed then."

He kissed her lips. "Later." He kissed her neck, her shoulder.

"Yes. Later."

Reality could have a turn later. She'd spend another hour in the fantasy.

CHAPTER ELEVEN

STAVROS idly wished he felt a sense of homecoming when he walked into the Kyonosian palace. He didn't. It felt like the walls had started to close in. A sensation he wasn't very fond of. Somehow, even the high ceiling seemed to reach down to him, as though it was trying to crush him.

Apt indeed.

He walked down the empty corridor and to his father's office. He pushed the door open. "Your Highness," he said, inclining his head.

"Stavros." His father stood, his hands clasped behind his back. "How was Greece?"

"Everything is in order. My hotels there are doing well."

"And your marriage?"

"Have I arranged it? Is that what you mean?"

"For all the money you've spent on that matchmaker I should think it would be settled by now," his father said, his voice gruff, his focus turned back to the papers spread over his desk.

Ah, yes, his matchmaker. His lover. The woman who held his body and his soul captive. The woman who made him feel more than any one person had ever made him feel in his life. The woman who made him question the core of his existence. That matchmaker.

He tightened his jaw. "Ms. Carter introduced me to several outstanding candidates."

"And?"

"And I've selected one." The words threatened to strangle him.

"Name?"

"Victoria Calder. She's English. Beautiful."

"Fertile?"

That made his stomach clench. "According to all of her paperwork, yes. That's part of why I hired Jessica. She handled that unpleasant pre-screening process for me. No potential scandals. No nasty medical surprises." It galled him to say the words. Because it made him feel no better than Jessica's ex. A man looking for a woman who met his terms. A man choosing a woman who was a mere placeholder, rather than a person.

Was that what he was? What he was doing?

Yes. It was.

"Excellent. When do you announce?"

"Not for a while." Not until he had to. Not until he'd taken the chance to draw out every possible moment with Jessica. "We'll make an appearance at Eva and Mak's ball."

"Excellent. I'm looking forward to it. This will be a good thing for, Kyonos. I'm certain of it."

"Yes," Stavros said, feeling no certainty at all.

Stavros nodded and exited the office. And fought the urge to punch the stone wall. Of course he was the only one to never disappoint his father. To never dishonor the Drakos name.

No, but his father had. His father had given up. Receded behind a veil of grief after his wife died. After he drove his oldest son away.

Stavros had never had the option of letting anyone down. He'd had to fix everything. Had had to pretend that everything in him was fixed because someone had to stand firm. He'd never had the luxury of feeling. Of falling apart.

He wanted to now. He wanted to give in to himself. He wanted to follow the emotions Jessica had brought back to him. Wanted to hold on to them forever.

He strode out of the palace and got into his car. He liked to drive himself whenever he could. He needed it. Because it was one of the few times he was able to be alone. When he was able to stop putting on a show.

Alone and with Jessica. Those were the only times that was possible. He shook his head and started the engine.

The streets in Thysius were crowded, but it didn't take long for him to get to his penthouse apartment. It was fortified with security, of course, but for the most part he didn't worry. Kyonos was a small country, and he'd always felt safe there.

He parked his car in the underground garage and touched his fingerprints to the scanner on the elevator. He would have to move into the palace eventually. But for now he would relish his freedom.

The doors to the lift slid open and revealed his penthouse, open and stark. It was a man's home, for sure. And it was modern in the extreme, his rebellion against the ultra old-fashioned stylings of the castle. One of his many small rebellions. Rebellions that, he could see now, were the lingering bits of a man he'd thought long banished. The man Jessica made him feel like again.

He looked on the couch and saw a cream-colored chenille blanket draped over the black leather. He smiled and picked it up, running his fingers over the soft fabric. There was a romance novel on the glass coffee table. He picked it up and flipped through a few pages, careful to save the spot it had been left open to.

"You're home."

He looked up and saw Jessica standing in the entryway of the living room and his breath stopped for a moment. She was so beautiful. She added something to his home, something soft and feminine, something it had been lacking. Something he'd certainly never thought it lacked before.

"Yes. How was your day?"

"Great. I spoke with Harneet on the phone for a while, and that was nice. Got an idea of the type of man she was looking for. I think I'm going to fly out and have lunch with her sometime during the weekend."

"The ball for Mak and Eva is coming up in a couple of weeks."

She nodded. "I know."

"Will you be there?"

"I... Probably not."

He nodded. "I wish you could be."

"Gee, not to hurt your feelings or anything, Stavros, but watching you make your public debut with Victoria ranks right up there with shoving glass under my fingernails for fun." She crossed her arms beneath her breasts and cocked her hip to the side.

"That isn't why I want you there."

"No? But that's what you'll be doing there. I know...I know that's what's going to happen. We both know. But that doesn't mean I want to watch it."

She turned away from him and he caught her arm. "Why are you suddenly mad at me?"

"For having all the sensitivity of a bull elk."

"I want you with me. If I could, I would fly to India with you and hover around the lunch table while you talked to Harneet. But I can't do that, can I? Because that's when the press would wonder, and since I am about to try and show that I'm making a move toward marriage we both know that can't happen."

"I know. So what do you want me to do at the ball? Hover around the edges and stare longingly at you?"

"No, I want you to hover around the edges so I can stare longingly at you."

She frowned. "That doesn't make any sense."

"None of this does. None of it. It hasn't from the moment I met you. You make me want things, Jessica. And I can't have any of them."

She closed her eyes. "Neither can I, Stavros."

"Jessica…"

"You know? I think I'm going to call Harneet and ask if I can meet with her earlier. I might leave tomorrow. I should be back in to help arrange any future endeavors with Victoria." She opened her eyes, her resolve clearly set, her chin pushed out at a stubborn angle.

"You're still helping me with Victoria?"

"It's my job, Stavros. And nothing changes that. Because nothing changes what has to happen."

"True enough." She was right. No matter what, he had to marry. And really, given her qualifications, Victoria was the woman he needed to marry. "I have to work early."

He knew what she was doing. Getting them both some distance. And they desperately needed it. They'd been in each other's pockets during their time in Greece, and she was staying in his home now. They needed space.

She nodded. "I'll probably be gone when you get home." She took a deep breath. "And I should probably sleep in my own room tonight."

He shook his head. "No. Sleep with me." Because even if they needed that kind of distance he wasn't sure he could stand it. "Please."

She nodded. "Okay."

Tomorrow they would take a break. He could clear his head.

He could set his focus back on what had to be done, and not on the insidious little fantasy that had burrowed beneath his skin over the past few weeks.

A fantasy that was simply impossible, no matter how badly he might want it.

Jessica felt like something that had washed up on the beach back at their Grecian villa by the time she got back from India a few days later. Definitely more bedraggled seagull than mermaid.

Their Grecian villa. What a silly way to think of it. It was Stavros's Grecian villa. She had simply shared his bed there for a while.

And now the idea was for her to share his penthouse for the next few weeks. She sighed. She'd done a lot of thinking on her out-of-town days, about whether or not what they were doing was a good idea.

The conclusion she'd come to was that it was a very bad idea, but then, she'd known it was a bad idea from moment one. They both had. They just hadn't been stronger than the desire.

She closed her eyes as she lifted her hand to the fingerprint reader on his elevator, one he'd programmed to accept her touch, and she knew that no amount of realization about the badness of their arrangement had made her any stronger.

She had a feeling Stavros was just as aware of the folly of it as she was. And that he was just as unlikely to stop.

She stepped inside and leaned her head against the metal wall as the doors slid closed and the lift carried her up the penthouse.

She'd strongly considered staying over in India for a while longer, if only to miss the ball. She didn't want to see Stavros with Victoria. She couldn't play disinterested party anymore. She couldn't separate Stavros her lover from Stavros her client. It was impossible.

Everything inside of her seemed to be tangled around him, and he seemed to be completely tangled up in her life.

The doors to the lift opened and she stepped out into his immaculate living room. She knew the housekeeper had been in, because if there was one thing she'd learned about Stavros, it was that his neat-as-a-pin modern-looking homes weren't kept in that fashion by him.

He left his clothes on the floor. And very often he left dishes in the sink.

He's not perfect.

No, he very much wasn't perfect, but she wasn't sure she cared about that, either. The reminder meant nothing, because if anything, being so aware that he wasn't perfect only gave validity to the feelings that were eating her from the inside out.

She stalked over to the fridge and pulled out a bottle of milk. It was nearly empty. She could add that to his list of sins. Putting a nearly empty milk bottle back into the fridge. And he'd probably forgotten to tell his housekeeper that he needed milk.

She padded down the hall and pushed open the door to his office. It was empty. He wasn't here.

It was easy to pretend, standing in his house, walking around as thought she belonged. Like they belonged together. But she'd had a lot of time to think while she'd been away. Even if she could have him, if he gave it all up for her...she couldn't let him.

Because she'd been the broken dreams of one man already. Stavros would only grow to resent her, too, as she tried, once again, to fit into a position she simply wasn't made for.

She took her phone out of her pocket and saw that she

had three new text messages. She'd put it on silent and forgotten about it.

She opened the first one.

Will you be back in time for dinner?

It was long past dinner so the answer to that was no.
She opened the next message.

Call me when you land so I know you're safe.

A smile curved her lips and she ran her fingers over the
screen of her phone. Why did he have to do things like that?
She scrolled to the next one.

Jess, I miss you.

A tear slid down her cheek. Had she really mourned
how hard it was for her to cry only a few weeks ago? Now
it seemed so easy. What had he done to her?

She curled her fingers around her phone and thought
about calling. She wasn't sure it was a good idea. In fact,
she was almost certain it was a bad idea. She would probably cry all over him. Maybe blurt out things she had no
business thinking, much less saying to him.

She hit the reply button and typed in: I miss you, too.
She deleted it. And took a breath.

I'm here. Where are you?

Her phone pinged a second later.

Can I send a car for you in an hour? I want to show you
something.

She'd wanted to rest for a while, but that didn't seem important anymore for some reason. The only thing that mattered was seeing him.

Sure. Give me time to get the travel grime off.

His return message came quickly. I'll be waiting for you.

CHAPTER TWELVE

THE car stopped in front of a lighthouse. The tower was dark, no signs of life anywhere in the small stone house. Jessica gathered up the skirt of her white, flowing gown, the one she'd purchased in Greece with Stavros in mind, and stepped out into the warm evening.

She looked up and saw Stavros, standing in front of the whitewashed building, his hands in his pockets, the top button of his shirt undone. He looked different. And so wonderfully the same. She had the strangest sense of being home. A feeling she hadn't had in so long she hadn't realized the absence of it.

"What's this?" she asked.

"A place I'd almost forgotten about. The palace is there," he said, pointing to glimmering lights on a hill. "Technically, this is part of the grounds. It hasn't been used for years. I used to come here whenever I could sneak away. I wanted to see it again and then, when I did…I wanted to show it to you."

"Why?" she asked, the tightness in her chest spreading, climbing into her throat, making it hard to breathe.

"Because you… Come with me, maybe then I can explain." He held his hand out and she took it, his fingers warm and strong as they closed around hers. He led her into the house. It was cool inside, the thick stone walls providing protection from the heat that still lingered in the air.

There was no furniture in the house. Not even a chair. "No one lives here?" she asked. "Well, that's actually obvious."

"No one has lived here in years. It's been vacant since I was a kid. Come with me." He led her through to the back of the house, to a small, rounded doorway with a steep set of stairs. She followed him up the curving staircase, her fingers laced with his.

They ended at the top of the tower, a small, clean room with a lantern at the center. Here there was a chair. And blankets laid across the floor.

"I used to come here and watch the ships," he said. "Imagine where they had been. Where they were going. Dream I was here, keeping them from hitting the rocks. Keeping watch."

"You've always been protecting people, haven't you?" she whispered.

He walked over to the lantern, pressing his hand against the glass case. "It was different. It wasn't real, first of all. And second…I remember caring more then for imaginary ships and dangers, feeling more for created peril, than I've cared about anything since. It was a child's game. Silly. But I had a passion for it. I felt something. I…I lost that. I lost it very purposefully. I…I wanted to show you, because I thought you might understand."

"If I ask what I'm supposed to understand does that mean I fail?" she asked, her heart pounding, her stomach weighted down. With desire. Fear. Longing.

"I want to feel again, Jess. For the first time since I was a child…I want it back. I want to care. You brought it back to me. Passion. I hadn't felt a passion for anything in so long…."

"Sure you have. I know you've had a lot of lovers besides me," she said, trying to steer the conversation away from where she feared it was going.

"Lust isn't the same as passion. It's not the same as... It's not the same as this. I used to think...I have thought for so long...that emotion was weakness. That caring for something, for someone, made you weak. And then I kept thinking of this place. Of how much I cared. Of how seriously I took even an imagined responsibility...because of love, really."

"Stavros..."

He moved to her, his eyes locked with hers. "You look like a goddess," he said, reverting to the physical. And she was so very glad he had.

"I had a layover in Greece and I remembered you saying... I remembered you saying I should wear a *pallas*. It's really vintage," she said, trying to force a smile. "Nearly a hundred years old, or so I was told."

He closed his eyes and leaned in, pressing his forehead to hers. She thought her heart might burst. "I need...I need you. Now."

His body was shaking with desire and that was something she could handle. This was what they both needed. The physical. To remember that this was about desire, mutual lust that they were both trying to satisfy.

It had been the reclamation of her sexuality. Of her body. A release of the things in her past, letting go of any remaining desire to be the person she had been. And she could never regret that. She wouldn't let herself.

She also wouldn't let it be more. There were so many things Stavros needed. So many responsibilities he needed a wife to help him fulfill. Things she couldn't possibly do.

"Are we... No one will come up here, right?"

"I told your driver he could leave. I drove myself." He

moved his hand to her hip, then slid it around to her lower back, to the curve of her bottom. "This dress is not fit for public. It's far too erotic."

"There isn't a single button on this dress to fuel your fantasies."

A strange expression crossed his face. "No. But I don't think it was ever the buttons." There was a heavy undertone to the statement, a meaning she didn't want to search for. Because there was no point. "I think it's been you all along."

She sucked in a sharp breath, ignoring the pain that lodge in her chest. This had to be about sex. Only sex.

If she let it be more…she just couldn't let it be more. Because it had to end.

"*You* have buttons, on the other hand." She put her hands on his chest and started working at the buttons of his dress shirt, revealing teasing hints of his perfect chest. She parted the fabric and slid her hands over his bronzed skin. "Oh, Stavros, I don't think I could ever get tired of this." The words were far too candid, far too honest, but she couldn't have held them back if she'd tried.

They were true. She could never tire of him. Not of his body, not of his humor, or his drive. Not of that spark of rebellion in him. That glorious bit of himself that could never be fully tamed.

She swallowed and pushed his shirt and jacket from his shoulders, leaving him nothing more than a pair of dark slacks.

He leaned in and pressed a kiss to her bare shoulder, his hand searching for where her dress was held together, at the waistband, taking the end of the fabric and tugging it from its secure place. He let it fall and she felt the top of the dress loosen.

He stepped back, his eyes appraising.

She put her hand on her shoulder and pushed the large

swath of fabric that crossed her body down, exposing her breasts to him. She watched his face as she slowly unwrapped herself, memorized the agony and ecstasy she saw there. No one had ever looked at her like that before. No one had ever made her feel so vulnerable and so powerful at the same time.

Stavros did it as effortlessly as most people drew breath.

He removed his pants and underwear quickly and shoved them to the side, naked and aroused for her enjoyment. And she did enjoy him. He was a sensual feast, amazing for all of her senses. To touch, to taste, to see. Stavros never disappointed.

She was about to go to him, to wrap her hand around his erection, but he moved first, dropping to his knees before her. He kissed her stomach, pushed her panties down and slid his finger through her slick folds, drawing the moisture from her body over her clitoris.

"You're so very good at that," she said, holding tightly to his shoulders. It was so much more than sexual skill, and she knew it.

Because her response to him went well beyond a basic physical reaction. It grabbed her, low and deep, and held her in thrall, no matter what was happening. Whether they were naked, alone on a beach, or fully clothed in a crowded ballroom, Stavros held her. All of her.

"The pleasure is mine," he said, rising back to his feet and kissing her mouth. "You have no idea."

He walked her backward to the blankets that had been spread on the floor, and held her tightly as he lowered them both to the soft surface.

"I've been expertly seduced," she said. "You planned this."

"I very much did," he said, not a hint of apology in his tone.

"One of the things I…" She stopped herself before she could say the words that were ringing inside of her head, her heart. "You and I think alike," she said. No feelings. No love. Oh, please not that.

He cupped her face and kissed her again while his other hand teased her breasts.

"You don't get to have all the fun," she said, sliding her hand down so that she could cup his erection.

He closed his eyes, the expression on his face one of a man completely given over to pleasure, completely lost in it. She memorized that, too. Watched him until her own pleasure became so intense she had to close her eyes.

She clung to the image of his face. Made sure it stayed in the forefront of her mind.

She clung to his shoulders, wrapped her leg around his hips, and he angled himself so that he slid inside of her. She bit her lip to keep from crying out. To keep from crying period.

He rolled her to her back and she parted her legs. He pushed in deeper and she arched into him, rocking her body in time with each of his thrusts.

There was no sound in the room beyond fractured gasps and short breaths, echoing from the stone walls. She dug her fingernails into his shoulders, trying to find something solid to keep her on earth. To keep her from losing herself completely.

If it wasn't already too late.

A sob climbed in her throat and burst from her as she fell over the edge, her orgasm stealing control of everything, drowning her in pleasure. She couldn't think, she could only cling to Stavros as wave after wave of bliss crashed down over her.

"Stavros," she said, tears spilling from her eyes.

He shuddered his own release, his muscles tight, her name on his lips.

After he pulled her against him, pressed kisses to her cheeks, her forehead, her mouth. His hands, hands that had been demanding in their pursuit and deliverance of pleasure, were gentle as he smoothed them over her curves.

She rested her head on his chest, tears drying on her cheeks, her eyes getting heavy in the aftermath of her release.

"I love you, Jess."

The words hit like a blow. She closed her eyes against the pain. Against the regret. Against the desire to turn and say them back to him. She couldn't. And he didn't mean it. He couldn't. He had responsibilities, responsibilities that far surpassed getting imaginary ships to the shore, and she knew that fulfilling those obligations meant the world to him.

And if he tried to put her in that position of being the one to fulfill them with…she could do nothing but fail. Could do nothing but watch the sweet tenderness in his eyes flatten into a cold, bitter hatred.

You're such a selfish bitch, Jessica. The words were always there. So easy to hear. So easy to remember.

She wouldn't be. Not now. No matter how much she wished she could. Tonight, though…she had to let herself have tonight.

She curled tighter into Stavros's embrace and hoped he wouldn't notice the tears that fell onto his chest.

Stavros knew the revelation should terrify him. But it didn't. Not even hours later, after he drove them back to his penthouse. After he laid her down in his bed and made love with her again. And now, as he lay in bed with Jessica curled up at his side.

He loved her.

He waited for something in him to crumble, for it to break and reveal his weakness. But it didn't. He felt reinforced. As though everything in Jessica, as though loving her, was shoring up his strength. Fueling it.

Love was different than he'd imagined. But then, Jessica was a different woman than he ever could have imagined.

He stroked her silky blond hair and watched her sleep, her cheek pillowed on his chest, and he wondered how he would ever face a future without her.

And he knew that if he was truly going to be the king, the man, he was meant to be, he needed her to be the one at his side.

CHAPTER THIRTEEN

It was the coward's way out. To sneak out while he was sleeping. While the first edges of light were peeking over the mountains. But men did it all the time, didn't they? And wasn't it supposed to save everyone from a big emotional scene? She certainly needed to be saved from it.

Because he'd said he loved her. Loving her, being with her, would stop him from finding everything he'd said he wanted. She would never, ever allow herself to be blamed for a man's ruined life and broken dreams.

Never again.

She held her suitcase tightly to her body and walked across the apartment, heading for the elevator.

"What are doing?"

She turned and saw Stavros, still naked, his pants in his hand.

"I'm...I'm going."

"Why?"

She let out a breath. "Because it was now or in a few weeks, and I decided it should be now. We both knew this wasn't permanent, and the four-week time frame no longer works for me."

"Put your suitcase down." He tugged his pants on quickly, leaving the belt undone.

She shook her head. "No. I'm leaving."

"I love you."

"You don't want love. You told me that already. You don't believe in it...you don't."

"I love you," he repeated, the words breaking.

"Stop it," she said, her voice shaking. "Just stop."

"It's true, I do. I love you, Jessica." He sounded tormented, his voice raw and pained. And she had caused it.

"It doesn't matter, don't say it like it does. Like it ever could. So you love me? What does that mean?"

"What does it mean? You want to know what it means? It means that my world stops turning when you aren't in it, and when I see you I feel like I can breathe again. That's what it means. It means I've found my passion again. That I'm not hollow anymore."

She dropped the suitcase then, pressing her hand to her chest. "No. What does it mean? Practically. In the real world. Because we both know that loving me doesn't make me able to have your royal babies, which means I'm not good enough to wear the royal crown. We both know it, so what's the point in any of this?"

"The point," he said, taking a step toward her, his expression deadly, "was to make me forget you. To make me get over this...need that I feel for you. To make it so the thought of a future without you didn't make me feel like my guts were being torn from my body. That was the point. We failed on all counts. I have...feelings, Jessica. I was so dead for so long and then you came into my life. And I couldn't put you at a distance, and I couldn't stop myself from being me when I was with you. I love you, and it's not simple, but it is so damned important because it changed me."

"You just think that, Stavros. Because of the sex. Because you love skirting the edge of convention as much as you possibly can and oh, how shocking would a divorced infertile queen be? But it's not real. It's temporary. Victoria is real. She can be your princess, your queen. And she can give you everything that you need. I can't."

"That is unfair, Jessica. Don't tell me what I feel."

"You would hate me in the end, Stavros. You would."

He stood there, his dark eyes pinned on her. "Tell me you love me, too."

She shook her head, the words tearing at her throat, struggling to escape. She wouldn't let them. She wouldn't make it worse.

He crossed the room in three strides, cupped her face, his hands so gentle, his expression so dark and fierce. "Tell me."

"No," she whispered, taking a step back and picking up her suitcase again. "I'm glad that you…found yourself with me, or whatever you want to call it. But you don't need me to feel passion. You don't need me to have emotions. I hope that things with Victoria go well. I hope you…I hope you love her some day." She didn't. She never wanted him to love her. She wanted his love forever, and if that made her small, she didn't care. But she would lie now. She would preserve what pride she had left now. "Please don't pay me. Not for any of it."

He didn't say anything, he only stood there, his body tense. He looked like he might try to physically stop her from leaving. But he didn't. He only watched her as she turned away. And she didn't look back. She couldn't.

Stavros could only watch as Jessica walked into the elevator, as the doors closed behind her. He could only concentrate on taking breaths, each one causing raw, physical pain.

She was wrong. She was wrong about everything. At least as far as he was concerned. He did need her. He needed her more than he needed air. She had brought something back to him. Something he'd long thought dead. Something he'd been glad was gone.

He hadn't allowed himself to feel the pain of his mother's

death. There had been too much to do. The people around him had fallen apart and his country had fallen into chaos. He had vowed he would never let that happen again.

But now…now he felt as though his insides had broken apart, that each breath dug a shard of the destroyed pieces into his flesh.

He looked at the wineglass sitting on the counter. Something Jessica must have had earlier. He walked to the kitchen area and released a growl as he picked up the glass and hurled it at the wall. It exploded into a million unfixable pieces.

And it didn't heal anything inside of him.

He feared nothing ever would.

CHAPTER FOURTEEN

STAVROS stood in front of his father's desk and looked down at the ring, nestled in a velvet box, glittering at him. The old-world vintage style of the piece mocked him. Made his heart feel as if it was shattering. Which should be impossible since it had shattered days ago.

"You have chosen then?" his father asked, looking at him from his seated position, his grey brows raised.

"Victoria is a wonderful choice for Kyonos. She will be a good queen." He reached out and curled his fingers around the box, lifting it from the desk. He raised it to his eyes, studied it.

"Your mother's ring," his father said. "She loved the unusual antique setting."

He laughed, a bitter sound. "I know a woman like that."

"I get the feeling she is not the woman you will be offering the ring to?"

Stavros shook his head. "Jessica Carter is not fit to be queen of Kyonos. Not by the standards set out for me. If I were to marry her, it would cause great scandal." Something in his chest burned, spread through his blood like fire. The thought of life without her, day after day, faded and brittle, devoid of color, of beauty.

"And if you weren't going to be king, Stavros?"

Stavros looked at his father. "But I am going to be king. And that means I have to think of more than just myself."

King Stephanos paused for a moment, his expression grave. "If you care for nothing, you'll never be able to care for your people. Not as you should."

"Love makes you weak," Stavros said. "I've seen it." He'd never condemned his father to his face. For some reason, now it poured from him. His renewed passion came with a renewal of every emotion. Happiness, and anger. Deep and hopeless sadness.

"What made me weak was the absence of love," his father said slowly. "I cared for nothing after your mother died. Not the country. Not even my children. And so I left it all abandoned. Which is easy to do when you no longer care."

Stavros had never seen it that way before. And yet, it rang true in his soul. Jessica made him feel real again. In touch as he hadn't been for years. She brought passion out in him, to be better, do better.

He looked at the ring again and an image flashed into his mind. One of him sliding the ring onto Jessica's finger. He tried to make the image turn into Victoria. He couldn't. There was only one vision for his future. Only one woman he could have at his side.

"If I marry Jessica there will be scandal," he said, his voice rough. "We will not have an heir. Her past will be fodder for the papers." He raised his focus to his father, who was regarding him silently. "And I don't give a damn. I love her. That's all that matters."

He turned away, his heart pounding hard.

"And that is why you will be twice the king that I have been, Stavros. You are a man who should follow his heart. Because your heart is strong."

He curled his fingers more tightly around the ring box. "It is now. Because of her."

* * *

"Jessica." She heard Stavros's voice through her hotel room door and she froze.

Why was he here? Why was he tormenting her? She'd been miserable for the past forty-eight hours. And she was planning on being miserable on the plane ride home. And then she was planning on being a sopping, miserable mess in North Dakota, so really, she didn't need his help.

Her entire body was heavy. The effort of dragging herself out of bed that morning had been nearly not worth it. Putting on pajamas last night hadn't been worth it, and she was still in yesterday's clothes because dressing hadn't seemed like it was worth it, either.

And now he was here. And she wanted to run to him and ignore reality so much it was nearly impossible to stop herself from flinging to door open and huddling against him.

"What do you want?" she said, knowing she sounded whiny and not caring. She felt whiny. She felt crushed.

"You. Open the door."

Her heart slammed against her breastbone. "Why?"

"Because I can tell you what it means now."

She swallowed and walked to the door, turning the dead bolt and unlinking the chain before pulling it open. "What?"

He gripped the edge of the door and the door frame. "I'm not marrying Victoria."

"What?" she asked again, taking a step back.

"I can't. I can't because you are the only woman that I want. I see you in my dreams, I see you when I'm awake and I close my eyes. I can't forget you. I don't want to forget you. I want you."

"But you…Victoria is perfect for you. She…she…" Jessica reached for her tablet computer, sitting on the arm of the couch, and swiped through a few screens until she found Victoria's file. "She is graceful, and wonderful and she can have your babies. She's beautiful and she does charities for homeless children. She's *perfect*."

"Yes, she is. There—" he pointed at her computer "—in writing, yes, she's perfect for my country. But you, Jessica Carter, you are perfect for me. And I don't care what you can't do, I only care what you do for me, what you give me. I care that when I'm with you I'm a better man. I have been closed off for years. What does it matter if I can give my people charm, an empty smile if I can give them nothing deeper than that? It doesn't matter. But you…you make me feel. You have forced me to find something in myself that's…real. To be more than a shell. I can't go back. I won't."

"Stavros, I… You can't do this. You can't. You have to have these things," she said, pointing to her computer again. "You have to. And if you don't…"

"If I don't, I'll be a better man for it. For pursuing what I want. For finding real passion. For ruling with everything I have in me. You, you helped me find it. Yes, I am expected to have a wife who can have heirs…but I won't. And that will have to be fine, it will be perfect, because my wife will be you. Unless you don't want me. Then…well, I'm not sure what I'll do then."

"Stavros—" her voice broke "—I want you. But I'm not going to be the cause of your unfulfilled vision. You want this so much. To be this perfect figurehead for your people. And I can't be the one to stop you from doing it. I've been that. I have been a man's broken dreams and I won't do it again. I can't. I can't watch love turn into resentment, and anger. I can't be more than I am. I am in this body, and I can only give so much."

A tear slid down her cheek, then another. Tears she realized had been stored up for the past few years of her life.

Anger and pain, and the anguish of being limited. Of not being enough.

Stavros moved to her, brushed her tears away with his thumb. "You are *everything*," he said, his voice rough. "You have given me everything. I didn't want love. Because I was so afraid of it, so afraid of the pain it could cause. Losing my mother devastated me. I just...shut down rather than dealing with it. I shut it all down. But you brought me back, you brought a part of me back and you restored it. I talked to my father. He told me the reason he let things fall apart was that he didn't care anymore. Not about anything. I wanted so badly not to be like him, not to lose myself to love, and I didn't realize I was him. Caring for nothing, going through the motions. But not now. Not since I met you."

He kissed her cheek. "Maybe on paper this doesn't work. But I don't think marriage is as simple as I believed it was. I can't just hire a wife the way I'd hire an assistant. I need a woman who will challenge me, who will push me, to be better, to do better. I know you are that woman. Most of all, I need the woman I love by my side."

"I love you," she said, letting the words come out. Finally. They felt like balm on her soul, healing old wounds that had never truly gone away. Until now. Until Stavros.

"I told you that once that you were enough of a dream for any man, and I stand by that statement now. I want nothing else. I want you."

She bit her lip. "I'm afraid you'll regret it. That you'll look at me every day and see...holes in me. All of the things I'm missing."

"Jessica, there are holes in me," he said, pressing his hand flat to his chest. "I am not perfect. But I believe you're the one who can fill the holes. The one who can make me stronger. Certainly the one who brings me joy."

She let out a sob. "I…I'm afraid you'll regret not having children."

"We can adopt children."

Shock bloomed in her stomach, making it hard to breathe. "But…adopted children couldn't take the throne, it doesn't solve the problem of heirs, it doesn't…"

"I'm not trying to solve a *problem* with adoption. If we want children, if we want to expand our family, we can adopt. We won't be the ones to produce the heirs. That's all right. I don't want another woman's children, I want yours. And by that I mean you're the one I want by my side raising my children. That's what matters anyway." He rested his forehead against hers. "That and if you love me. Because if you really love me, then nothing else matters."

"I do. I really do love you. But when we met you told me all the things you wanted and…"

"Because I was scared. A coward. I was trying to make things easier on myself. Going through life without caring is vain, but it's simple. I was going to marry a woman who would have been a placeholder, and you'll never be that. You make me want to be the king, the man, I didn't know I could be. You make me strong. Be my wife, Jessica. Please."

Every word, every line in his face, spoke of his sincerity. And if she thought back to their time, to the moment they'd first met, she knew it had started then. That every look, every touch, every kiss, had brought them to this point.

That every bit of pain before they met, had made them strong enough to stand here. Made them strong enough to make marriage work. To have love that lasted.

"I… Yes." Her heart lifted, happiness, true happiness, filling her, flooding her. Every place inside of her that had felt empty, incomplete, seemed filled now, with love.

"Don't ever feel like you aren't enough for me. You fill me. All the empty places in me."

She nodded. "I believe you."

"Jessica, this life won't always be easy. There will be press to deal with, and there are big responsibilities, long work hours and a lot of traveling. But I want you by my side for all of it. My queen, my lover, my partner."

"Yes," she said again, her voice stronger this time. "Stavros, I've loved before. But this is different. Because I feel like you're a part of me. I feel like you want me, and not me wrapped up as part of a dream, a fantasy. I truly believe that you love me, and not who you wish I was."

"I do. You aren't a dream. Far from it."

"Hey!" she said, laughing through her tears.

"What I mean is, you are too special, too unique for me to ever have dreamed up. I wrote down all the things I thought I needed in a wife, and I was delivered something completely different. I didn't truly know myself at all, or what I needed. Not until I met you."

"I must be the worst matchmaker in the world. I matched a woman to a prince and then…and then I got engaged to him. We are engaged, right?"

"Yes, we are. In fact—" he reached into his pocket and pulled out a white satin box "—this was my mother's." He opened the box and revealed a platinum, pear-cut diamond with intricate detail etched into the band. "It's been in our family for hundreds of years. When I saw it…when I saw it I knew there was only one woman I could give it to. It's perfect for you."

"You're right," she said. "You're so very right."

He took her hand in his and slid the ring onto her third finger. "It's like it was made for you."

She shook her head. "No, I think you were made for me."

Jessica leaned in and kissed him, pouring all of her love into the kiss. Now that she had Stavros, she didn't feel like she was missing anything.

"You fill all those places inside me that used to feel empty," she whispered.

He stoked her hair, his touch so warm and perfect. Even more perfect now that she knew she would have him forever. "As you do for me. I think you must have been my missing piece."

She closed her eyes and leaned into him. "For so long I felt like I was made wrong."

"No, *agápe mou,* you weren't made wrong. You were made for me."

* * * * *

#3117 IN THE HEAT OF THE SPOTLIGHT
The Bryants: Powerful & Proud
Kate Hewitt
Ambitious tycoon Luke Bryant's power and passion will lay scandalous Aurelie bare.... She's determined not to let him get beneath her skin, but faced with the sexiest man she's ever met, Aurelie can't resist just one touch!

#3118 NO MORE SWEET SURRENDER
Scandal in the Spotlight
Caitlin Crews
Ivan Korovin's only solution to a PR nightmare created by outspoken Miranda Sweet is to give the ravenous public what they want—to see these two enemies become lovers! But soon the mutually beneficial charade becomes too hot to handle!

#3119 PRIDE AFTER HER FALL
Lucy Ellis
Lorelai is an heiress on the edge, hiding her desperation behind her glossy blond hair and even brighter smile. Legendary racing driver Nash Blue never could resist a challenge—and he begins his biggest yet: unwrapping the real Lorelai St James....

#3120 LIVING THE CHARADE
Michelle Conder
When buttoned-up Miller Jacob needs to find a fake boyfriend, Valentino Ventura, maverick of the racing world, is the last person she wants. Up for the job, Valentino can't wait to help Miller let her hair—and whatever else she wants—down!

EXPHPCNM0113RB

REQUEST YOUR FREE BOOKS!

2 FREE NOVELS PLUS
2 FREE GIFTS!

YES! Please send me 2 FREE Harlequin Presents® novels and my 2 FREE gifts (gifts are worth about $10). After receiving them, if I don't wish to receive any more books, I can return the shipping statement marked "cancel." If I don't cancel, I will receive 6 brand-new novels every month and be billed just $4.30 per book in the U.S. or $4.99 per book in Canada. That's a saving of at least 14% off the cover price! It's quite a bargain! Shipping and handling is just 50¢ per book in the U.S. and 75¢ per book in Canada.* I understand that accepting the 2 free books and gifts places me under no obligation to buy anything. I can always return a shipment and cancel at any time. Even if I never buy another book, the two free books and gifts are mine to keep forever.

106/306 HDN FVRK

Name	(PLEASE PRINT)	

Address		Apt. #

City	State/Prov.	Zip/Postal Code

Signature (if under 18, a parent or guardian must sign)

Mail to the **Harlequin® Reader Service:**
IN U.S.A.: P.O. Box 1867, Buffalo, NY 14240-1867
IN CANADA: P.O. Box 609, Fort Erie, Ontario L2A 5X3

**Are you a current subscriber to Harlequin Presents books
and want to receive the larger-print edition?
Call 1-800-873-8635 or visit www.ReaderService.com.**

* Terms and prices subject to change without notice. Prices do not include applicable taxes. Sales tax applicable in N.Y. Canadian residents will be charged applicable taxes. Offer not valid in Quebec. This offer is limited to one order per household. Not valid for current subscribers to Harlequin Presents books. All orders subject to credit approval. Credit or debit balances in a customer's account(s) may be offset by any other outstanding balance owed by or to the customer. Please allow 4 to 6 weeks for delivery. Offer available while quantities last.

Your Privacy—The Harlequin® Reader Service is committed to protecting your privacy. Our Privacy Policy is available online at www.ReaderService.com or upon request from the Harlequin Reader Service.

We make a portion of our mailing list available to reputable third parties that offer products we believe may interest you. If you prefer that we not exchange your name with third parties, or if you wish to clarify or modify your communication preferences, please visit us at www.ReaderService.com/consumerschoice or write to us at Harlequin Reader Service Preference Service, P.O. Box 9062, Buffalo, NY 14269. Include your complete name and address.

When Selene asks her father's most hated business rival for help, she has no idea what it will cost her! Read on for a scintillating sneak-peek from USA TODAY bestselling author Sarah Morgan's incredible new book, SOLD TO THE ENEMY.

* * *

STEFAN stared at her, his eyes sweeping her face for clues and suddenly he stilled. Those beautiful washed-green eyes were a rare color he'd seen only once before. "Selene? Selene Antaxos."

"You *do* recognize me."

"Barely." His eyes swept her frame. "You've…grown." He remembered her as an awkward teenager completely dominated by her overprotective father. A pampered princess never allowed out of her heavily guarded palace.

Stay away from my daughter, Ziakas.

Just thinking of the name Antaxos was enough to ruin his day, and now here was the daughter, standing in his office.

Dark emotion rippled through him, unwelcome and unwanted.

He reminded himself that the daughter wasn't responsible for the sins of the father.

"Why are you dressed as a nun?"

"I had to sneak past my father's security."

"I can't imagine that was easy. Of course if your father didn't make so many enemies, he wouldn't need an entire army to protect him." Blocking the feelings that rose inside him, he stood up and strolled round his desk. "What are you doing here?"

She bent down and caught hold of the hem of her habit.

"Do you mind if I take this off? It's really hot and there's no point in keeping it on now I'm safe with you."

Knowing that most women considered him anything but "safe," Stefan watched in stunned disbelief as she wriggled and struggled until finally she freed herself, emerging with her hair in tangled disarray. Underneath she was wearing a white silk shirt teamed with a smart black pencil skirt that hugged legs designed to turn a man's mind to pulp.

"Does your father know you're here?"

"What do you think?" The corner of her mouth dimpled into a naughty smile, and Stefan stared, hypnotized by her lips, trying to clear his mind of wicked thoughts.

"I think your father must be having a few sleepless nights."

Come into my house, Little Red Riding Hood, and close the door behind you.

* * *

Can Selene deal with the devil and escape unscathed?
Find out what happens when the door closes behind
Selene on January 22, 2013, from Harlequin Presents®!

HPEXP0113